DOROTHY CLAES

A N D   T H E

PROWL OF THE YULE CAT

THE SILVER FOX MYSTERIES
BOOK TWO

C.P. MORGAN

Ordering Information:
www.authorcassandramorgan.com
www.amazon.com

First Printing: October 2018
White Whisker Publications

ISBN: 978-1-732138-7-9

Special Thanks to

*Sandra Hults, Robin Madigan, Quasar Morris,
Cassiopeia Mulholland, Heidi Herman,
Dísa Bjarna and Su Opansky.*

með allri ást minni

A NOTE FROM THE AUTHOR

Research for an author is both a boon and a bane. We'll spend six hours looking up the type of gravel used in a driveway for a middle-class, American family living in New Jersey during the 1970's, and then we'll forget that the family's Buick didn't come in that particular color for that year.

When I started this series, I knew I would have to rely on experts beyond what my web browser could provide me. So, when it came to Icelandic dialogue, I handed my rough draft to those experts who both spoke and lived in Iceland.

I was surprised that most of my English-to-Icelandic translations hadn't been too terrible. But when it came to my Icelandic characters speaking English to dear Dorothy, that was where I had failed.

Contractions, you see, are a tricky thing. For the older generations, the use of contractions when speaking English was almost non-existent. But with the advancements of technology, the internet, and in the influences of American and British television, music and movies, the younger generations picked up on the use of contractions with ease.

I ask that you please keep this in mind as you read, and imagine you are in Iceland alongside Dorothy and Solomon, helping them to solve the case. The English dialogue you read is as true a representation as possible to what it would sound like to speak English with a native Icelander.

Happy Reading!

Love,
~ Cassie

ONE

THE BELL ABOVE THE DOOR TO RICHARD'S
Anecdotes chimed brightly. Louisville, Massachusetts's
wizened postman stepped through, stomping his
boots and brushing snow from his wiry gray hair.

"Hello, Mr. Altman," Aaron said from behind the
glass counter.

The postman glanced around the little antique shop,
then trudged toward the young man before him.

"Hello, Aaron. Is Ms. Claes around by chance?"
The man licked his lips and tried to peer into the back
room.

"She's upstairs at the moment, sir," Aaron said,
holding out his hand for the mail.

Mr. Altman grunted and reached into his bag. "That
cursed cat still with her?" he spat.

Suddenly, the avocado-green door that led to the

upper apartments opened. A black cat bounded down the steps and began circling the postman's ankles. Mr. Altman tried to nudge the cat away, but the little cat was persistent in rubbing against him.

"Yes, Solomon is still here," Aaron said, his hand still held out for the mail.

Mr. Altman tried to set the mail in Aaron's hand but missed. Aaron caught the stack of envelopes, bringing the wizened man's attention back to him.

"How's school going?" asked Mr. Altman. He licked his lips again, looking up the stairs for Dorothy.

"It's my final year, sir," said Aaron, puffing out his chest with pride.

"That's wonderful. Congratulations. Are you spending your Christmas break with your family? I'm sure anywhere would be warmer than here at the moment."

Aaron nodded and began sorting through the envelopes for Dorothy's personal mail and those for the shop.

"My family is from Jamaica, sir. I'm looking forward to visiting the gran market. It's been years since I've been back." The young man's eyes sparkled as he spoke, but Mr. Altman took no notice.

His attention had turned to the shop's owner, Dorothy Claes, as she stepped off the floral-carpeted stairs.

"Well, don't let this little fox work you to death," the postman said, chuckling.

Dorothy's head snapped around, and the postman winked, giving her a flirty nod.

"Oh, no, sir," Aaron said, handing Dorothy the now-sorted pile of mail. "Ms. Claes is very generous with my studies."

Dorothy smiled and accepted the stack. "Thank you, Aaron," she said.

Solomon gave Mr. Altman's shin one last head bonk, then trotted toward the front window. He stretched and kneaded a purple pillow embroidered with an intricate S.

"Well, g'day, Aaron. Ms. Claes." Mr. Altman pulled up his hood in preparation to face the harsh December snow and headed back into the cold.

Dorothy shuddered as she watched him close the door. "That man is barking up the wrong tree," she whispered under her breath.

"He means well, Ms. Claes," said Aaron with a shrug.

"Mmm, yes, and so does a snake until it gets hungry," Dorothy muttered as she continued to sift through the mail as Aaron laughed. "You're too good, Aaron." Her eyes landed on a small envelope. The word CONFIDENTIAL was stamped in red across its front. She tore into the envelope, pulling out the single piece of paper.

"It looks like another letter came from Karlee," Aaron said, a smirk slowly forming across his face. "And one from Mr. Red."

Dorothy raised an eyebrow at her assistant. "I take it back. You're not that good."

"Mr. Red is a wonderful man," Aaron said, throwing his hands up and failing to keep his smirk from forming into a full-fledged smile.

"Have you finished inventorying those 15th-century coins we received yesterday?"

Aaron shifted uncomfortably. "No, ma'am. I – I'll get right on it." He turned toward the back room, his dreadlocks bouncing as he hurried away.

Solomon pounced at the falling snow outside the window, then took off after Aaron with a series of chirps.

Dorothy shook her head and returned her attention to the letter before her.

To Ms. Dorothy Virginia Shirley Claes,

This notice is in regard to your request pertaining to the release of health records concerning the late Richard Van Damme.

This is to inform you that the aforementioned file has been classified as sealed by the United States Department of Inquiry.

This is the only and final notice you will receive.

Dorothy clenched her teeth. She stuffed the letter back into the envelope and slammed the pile of mail on the counter.

Aaron slid his chair back, craning his neck to look at her from the backroom.

"Everything all right, ma'am?" he asked.

Dorothy rubbed her temples. "Yes, thank you."

There was a pause as Dorothy stared at the incriminating envelope before her. It had taken her nearly a year to track down the correct departments to write to about her father's health records. Destin had been absolutely no help. Now, she was back at square one.

"Ma'am, I think some of these coins are going to need to soak overnight," Aaron said gently.

Dorothy sighed. "I'll take a look before you do so. Sometimes they just need a bit of elbow grease." She forced a smile and moved the envelope to the back of the pile.

"Yes, ma'am," Aaron said, and Dorothy heard the squeak of his chair as he returned to his work.

A gust of wind pulsed against the large glass windows, sending a swirl of powdery snow into the air. Solomon darted from the backroom. He leapt onto his purple pillow, front paws plastered to the window and watched until the wind died.

He turned back to Dorothy, his green eyes still dilated with excitement.

"What?" Dorothy asked him, a smile pulling at her lips. "It's too cold for you to play outside right now. We'll go for a walk in a few days."

Solomon snapped back with a single, curt mew and jumped onto the counter. Dorothy pressed her forehead between the cat's ears before scooping him up and scratching his chin.

"I'm sure Red's enjoying himself," she whispered to Solomon. "Should we go visit him in Australia again, hmm? You can play with Ruby again."

Solomon purred loudly as Dorothy set him back on the counter and picked up Karlee's and Red's letters.

The cat sniffed the envelopes and meowed incessantly until Dorothy had pulled out Karlee's letter and allowed him to rub and roll on the now empty envelope.

Dear Ms. Dorothy,

How are you? How's Solomon? Are you guys

coming to the cat show in Paris again next month?
I hope you do! We all miss you so much!

*Jenna wanted me to tell you that you and
Solomon can share a hotel room with her. I
wouldn't, though. Don't tell her I said it, but she
snores really loud.*

*Scott and I have finally picked a wedding date,
so we hope you can come! He wanted to have the
wedding in Giza, but I told him I had had enough
of Egypt for a while.*

*I also wanted to tell you that I got accepted into
the forensics program! You really inspired me to
figure out what kind of career I want, and I really
want to help solve cases and stuff. Like you.*

Anyway, I hope you and Solomon are well!

Votre amie dévouée,

Karlee

Dorothy smiled and wrestled the envelope away
from Solomon.

"What is –?" She stopped putting the letter back into
the envelope, noticing Karlee had sent several large
catnip leaves along. She pulled one out and handed it
to Solomon before picking up Red's letter.

My Dorothy,

The summer days are growing longer here, which means winter must be holding you desperately hostage. I can only imagine you wrapped in a comforter against the cold. How I would very much like to wrap you in my arms and warm you myself, much like how we found each other in Tulsa. That is if Solomon will ever let me get close to his dear mommy. Ruby had her pups a few weeks ago, so perhaps we can distract him with keeping the litter out of trouble.

I just returned from South Africa, and I sincerely want to thank you for your help. It's a shame D won't let us work together more often. Please tell me how I may repay you. I am no Parisian chef, but I can assure you, the steak is fresh – very fresh.

Give Solomon a scratch from me. I await your return to the ranch with baited breath.

All my love,

Red

Dorothy swallowed and felt her cheeks flush as she read Red's letter again. The chime of the bell as the front door opened was the only thing that pulled her attention away.

"Can I help you?" she asked her customer, trying to rub the heat from her cheeks.

"Uh, yeah. Are you Miss Class?" a plump woman asked, snapping her gum and clicking her long, painted nails together.

"It's Claes. Like case but with an L. But, yes. What can I do for you today?"

The woman rolled her eyes at Dorothy's correction and snapped her gum again. "I called earlier about that painting?"

Dorothy nodded. "I'll have Aaron bring it in for us." She tucked Red's letter into the pocket of her cardigan and reached for a pair of white gloves.

"Yeah, okay," the woman replied, popping her gum again. Dorothy plastered what she hoped looked like a smile on her face. The woman had called looking to make a quick buck at the expense of her grandmother's recent death. Not that she looked like she needed the money. The woman could have given Miss Kitty a run with all the furs she wore.

Solomon approached the woman and sniffed at her designer knockoff boots.

The woman gasped and crouched so quickly, Solomon's fur stood on end.

"Oh, my gracious! She's so precious. Oh, come here, darling!" the woman cooed, holding out her arms to the bewildered cat.

Solomon sniffed at her claw-like nails and took off

for the backroom.

"He's a bit particular about who he likes," Dorothy said, the smile on her face beginning to numb her cheeks.

"Well, that's no way to treat a customer." The woman scoffed and crossed her arms.

"Is the painting in your vehicle, ma'am?" Aaron asked, saving Dorothy from the retort that was forming on the tip of her tongue.

"Um, yeah." The woman gave Aaron a hard look. "Here. It's in the backseat." She held her keys out for him. "Don't go stealing anything while you're in there!"

Dorothy bit her tongue. The woman ended up huffing over her offer. The painting wasn't an original as the woman had been led to believe. Dorothy was more than happy to give a polite goodbye and chuckled when the woman's heel became stuck in a chunk of ice as she climbed into her car. Even Solomon relaxed again, resting his head on his paws by the window.

Her workday seemed to be growing longer as the darkness of winter came sooner with each passing night. The wind whipped relentlessly, a precursor to the storm that was on its way. With a relieved sigh, she turned the sign hanging from the door to Closed.

"You're not walking home in this," she said as

Aaron bundled up against the cold.

"I'll be all right, ma'am," he assured her, wrapping a second scarf around his face. Solomon batted at the tassels that hung from the ends before Aaron stuffed them into his jacket.

Dorothy shook her head and pulled out her cell phone. "Humor an old woman. I'm calling you a cab."

Aaron didn't argue. Instead, he pulled his scarf from his jacket and dangled it in front of the cat. Solomon pounced on the scarf so vivaciously, he nearly choked Aaron in the process.

As soon as Dorothy had seen Aaron off, she locked the door behind her and set a kettle on in her little apartment above the shop.

Solomon wound around her ankles, chirping and meowing until she opened a tin of food and plopped it in his bowl. She reached for her joint cream and carefully lowered herself into the single armchair, flicking on the television.

"And here's another look at the live weather doppler 2000. Look at that snow band coming through here, folks! I'm guessing another two inches by morning," the newscaster exclaimed excitedly. "Flights have been canceled all across the country as The Little Blizzard That Could continues to barrel its way through the United States."

Dorothy rolled her eyes. Had no one on the East Coast experienced snow before? She recapped the tube of joint cream and flicked the television off. Solomon jumped into her lap, still licking canned food from his whiskers. She pulled Red's letter from her pocket, and Solomon immediately began rubbing on the envelope.

My Dorothy
The summer days are

Dorothy's phone vibrated between her hip and the chair cushion. She started, sending Solomon to the floor. She quickly fished out the phone and answered.

"Hello?"

"Fennec," came Destin's urgent voice.

Dorothy chewed her tongue. "It's Dorothy," she corrected. "I'm glad you called. I need to speak to you about my father's health records." She began pacing anxiously before the bookcase that led to the secret room beneath her shop.

"I'm sorry, Fennec. There's no time –"

"Why are my father's health records sealed? And what is the United States Department of Inquiry?"

"Fennec, I need to deploy you in the field immediately," Destin continued.

"I'm not going anywhere until you tell me why I can't see my father's health records."

Solomon meowed defiantly from the floor in front of Dorothy as if agreeing with her.

Destin sighed. "Fennec, Caprice is missing."

Dorothy stopped. "What do you mean, missing?"

"She hasn't checked in for two days. I've uploaded what we have to your Fox Den app. I hope you're able to dress warmly."

Destin paused, but Dorothy did not immediately answer. She looked at Solomon, who pawed at her pant leg, his large green eyes staring at her with concern.

"Destin, I'm not going anywhere until you release my father's health records to me."

Destin sighed. "Fen – Dorothy, all of our other agents are on assignment. I have no one else to send. I cannot release Richard's health records. I don't have the authority to do –"

"But you know who does," Dorothy snipped.

"Caprice could be captured, injured or worse. What's more important? Someone's life, or information about someone who's already dead?"

Destin's words cut through Dorothy, and Solomon gave a mournful mew.

Dorothy cleared her throat. "All right, but there's a nasty storm here on the East Coast. Flights are canceled everywhere."

"I'm well aware. Artie will get you safely there. I'm sending a taxi in an hour."

"An hour?"

"You can pack in an hour, can't you, Fennec?" Destin's usually playful tone was harsh and worried.

Dorothy huffed and pulled the phone away from her ear. "Oh, Fennec," Destin called as Dorothy's thumb poised above the End Call button. She returned the phone to her ear. "For your own safety, please leave your father in the past."

The phone clicked, and Dorothy felt her stomach drop.

TWO

DOROTHY TOSSED HER SUITCASE ON THE bed with one hand, the other precariously balancing her phone. Solomon immediately jumped in, his tail hanging out the side.

"Mary Pat, I have something important to tell you," Dorothy said to her sister.

"Did Red propose? Oh, please tell me Red proposed!"

"What? No. Mary Pat, this is –"

"Dorothy, that man's been stringing you along for a year! If you were twenty again, you wouldn't stand for this."

Dorothy shoved her entire stock of thermal underwear into the suitcase, removing Solomon before she turned back to her dresser.

"What I choose to tolerate in my love life is my own

business," she said.

"So, you finally admit you're in love with him."

Dorothy buried her face in a night dress. She stuffed it in her suitcase and removing Solomon once more.

"Fine, I love him. Are you happy now?" Dorothy could almost hear her sister's eyes narrowing and the corner of her mouth curling.

"Only if you are, dear."

"Mary Pat, I need you to do something for me. It's about Daddy."

"The estate's been settled, Dory-dear."

"It's about his health records. I need you to look up the United States Department of Inquiry. Write that down. Are you writing this down?"

"Yes, yes. United American States Bureau of Inquisition."

Dorothy heard buttons being pushed on a microwave in the background.

"Mary Pat, you're not listening! They won't release Daddy's health records!" Dorothy pulled Solomon out of her suitcase once more and zipped it tight before remembering her toiletries and unzipping it again in frustration.

"Dorothy, Dad's been gone for over a year. It's time to let him rest."

"Dad is resting under ten feet of soil. My mind is

not. Will you please do this for me? The United States _"

"Department of Inquiry. Yes, I'll see what I can find."

Dorothy zipped up her suitcase once more and heaved it into the living room. She had packed enough warm clothes to last a lifetime, and the sides of her suitcase bulged.

"Thank you. Call me as soon as you know something, all right?"

The microwave beeped loudly through the phone, and Dorothy could hear the clanking of silverware.

"I will. Now, you tell that man to get a move on it. Sleep well, dear!"

Dorothy hung up before Mary Pat could think of something more to say. Outside, a car honked its horn. Dorothy swung on her coat and lugged her suitcase to the waiting taxi outside.

Large flakes of snow beat against the taxi as the driver pulled onto the road. Dorothy felt the car slide and hurried to buckle her seatbelt. She pulled out her phone, keeping one cautious eye on the road from the back seat.

She dialed Aaron's number and waited.

"Hello?" came her assistant's concerned voice.

"Aaron, it's Dorothy," she said.

"Is everything all right, ma'am?"

"I've been called away unexpectedly." Dorothy hated lying to Aaron, but protocols for the Silver Foxes forbade her from telling him anything about the organization. "I'm leaving you in charge of the shop for a few days. It shouldn't be too busy for you, but if the county's still under a weather emergency in the morning, I want you to stay home, understand?"

"Yes, ma'am. Is Solomon with you again?"

Dorothy sighed. She hadn't said goodbye to the little cat before leaving. "No, he's in the apartment. Would you mind feeding him for me? I left him enough kibble to get him through a few days, but you know how he is about his canned food."

"Of course, ma'am," Aaron said with a yawn.

"He gets one tin of it in the morning and one at night. They're in the cupboard above the sink."

"I'll take care of him," said Aaron.

"I'm sure you will, but don't go sneaking him broccoli again."

Aaron chuckled. "I won't, ma'am. Promise. Be careful."

"I will. Thank you, Aaron. Have a good night."

Dorothy spent the next two hours clutching the handle assist above the window of the door with one hand and the suitcase beside her with the other. The taxi fishtailed more than once, as did the vehicles on the highway all around them. When they finally reached the airport, Dorothy vaulted out of the car, her hands still trembling.

She dragged her massive suitcase behind her and approached the woman at the counter, handing her the Silver Fox passport.

"Hello, again, Ms. Fennec," the woman said brightly. "Right this way."

She led Dorothy down the familiar, quiet hall. "Some storm, i'n'it?" she asked, smiling again, and Dorothy caught sight of a smear of bright pink lipstick across her front tooth.

"It certainly is," Dorothy replied.

"We've canceled all our flights. Everyone around here has. You're very brave, Ms. Fennec," the woman said.

"Or foolish," Dorothy muttered.

The woman approached a heavy metal door and slid her badge through the card reader. The door clicked, and the woman held the door open.

"Thank you," Dorothy said, then paused at the threshold. "You may want to check your lipstick," she whispered.

The suitcase handle jumped from Dorothy's hand and stood upright on its wheels. Dorothy and the airport attendant stared at the case. The woman laughed, holding her hand up to her mouth.

"Thanks," she said, then hurried back up the hall.

Dorothy reached for her suitcase again. The weather had to be playing havoc on her joints for her to lose her grip on the handle without realizing it.

"Artie?" she called, her voice echoing throughout the plane hangar.

"I'm here!" Artie called, emerging from beneath the Learjet. "Some weather, eh?" he asked, wiping grease from his hand and extending it to Dorothy.

"Are you sure it's safe to fly?" Dorothy asked. "Every other flight is delayed –"

A smile spread across Artie's weathered face. He tapped his finger against his nose, silencing Dorothy. "They're not flying with ol' Artie in a Silver Fox-commissioned jet."

Dorothy narrowed her eyes. "A Silver Fox commission?"

Artie nodded and reached a hand for Dorothy's suitcase. "This bird's got more than a few tricks up her sleeve. Don't worry Ms. Fennec. You're in safe hands."

The suitcase jumped from Artie's hand, and the sides began to bulge. Artie took a cautious step back, but Dorothy lunged for the zipper. A furry black head popped through the hole. Solomon pushed himself through, hackles raised and hissing and spitting at everything in sight.

Dorothy pulled the cat into her arms as a plume of fur flew into the air. Artie took another step back and sneezed violently.

"Solomon!" Dorothy said, trying to lay the cat's fur flat. "How did you-you poor thing."

Artie sneezed again and pulled a handkerchief from his pocket. Solomon wiggled free of Dorothy's grip and landed at the man's feet, grooming himself furiously.

"I need to get him back," said Dorothy. "I can't take him with me."

Artie sniffed and looked at his watch, his eyes looking more bloodshot by the moment. "There's no time. We have a flight plan we need to stick to. He'll just have to come with –" He sneezed again.

Solomon shook his head as Artie's spray showered over him. He rubbed against the man's legs and meowed up at him.

"I didn't know you were allergic to cats," said Dorothy.

"If I know I'm going to be around them, I can take something, but –"

Dorothy pulled out her phone. She had no carrier,

or even Solomon's leash and harness. Aaron would surely be asleep by now, and Mary Pat couldn't navigate a city block in bright sunlight, let alone drive hours on the highway in a snowstorm.

Artie blew his nose and pulled an inhaler from his pocket. "We have to go, Dorothy. If Solomon can survive a brush with a guardian of the dead, he'll be just fine in Iceland." He took a breath on his inhaler, then picked up Dorothy's suitcase and headed for the plane.

Solomon wound himself around Dorothy's ankles, mewing and purring. She glared down at him, pocketing her phone and following Artie. Solomon trotted up the steps of the plane ahead of her and plunked himself immediately on one of the window seats.

"You're so proud of yourself, aren't you?" she asked, taking her own seat. Solomon's bright green eyes turned on her, and he blinked before resuming his study of the hangar out the little window.

Several minutes later, Dorothy found herself watching the swirling snow whiz past the windows, but the turbulence she expected never came. A small screen unfolded itself from the ceiling, and Artie's red-eyed and swollen face stared back at her. She pulled a pair of headphones from the side compartment and plugged them into the port in the arm of her chair.

"Did Destin tell you anything about your mission?" Artie asked through a stuffy nose.

Dorothy shook her head. "Only that Caprice is missing. I didn't even know we were going to Iceland until you mentioned it."

Artie furrowed his brow. "That's odd," he muttered as he shrugged.

"I'll brief you on what I know from taking Caprice there. If you can, find her case files, unless all her belongings went missing too." The man sighed, his eyes staring into the distance for a moment. "Caprice is one of our best agents. She came on just before me. If she's gone missing..." He trailed off, his eyes unfocused again.

"I'll find her, Artie," Dorothy whispered.

Artie straightened again. He sniffed and resumed his typical demeanor. "A few weeks ago, there were reports of children going missing in the town of Eskifjorður. The locals believe it's one of the fabled creatures from their mythology. Icelanders believe fairies and giants are as real as their father or neighbor. But a pattern started to emerge. It was always the eldest daughter who went missing. Caprice is a professional storyteller and a tour guide in Cape Agulhas. Her knowledge of mythology from all over the world is unsurpassed by anyone we know. That's why Destin sent her. What she's found since then or communicated with Destin, I don't know."

"Is there any connection between the daughters or the families of the girls who've gone missing?"

"Well, they're probably all blonde," said Artie with a grin. Dorothy shot him a look through the little screen, and the man winked at her before wiping his nose.

"Can I access the internet from here? Maybe I can do some research before we land. Or can I make a call?"

"Sorry, Ms. Fennec. In order to keep the plane stable through this wind, I've had to activate the – well, it's an artifact. It's complicated. But it interferes with certain radio frequencies, including any kind of phone or internet connection. The internal network of the plane is shielded from its effects by a special alloy in the outer hull. We can still speak here, but I'm afraid that unless you already downloaded the files to your devices, you're going to have to wait until we land."

"I thought we were supposed to neutralize artifacts and remove them. How many artifacts does Destin have in use?"

Artie shrugged. "I'm not sure. We've been using the Dropa stones for our planes since before I was an agent. I know Destin uses some sort of device that keeps kinetic and potential energy in constant flux, so our headquarters are unaffected by any artifacts inside or out."

Dorothy's mind drifted to the secret passage in her apartment. It led to a room full of artifacts her father had collected over the years, and it seemed a safe bet that other agents had artifacts hidden away as well.

Artie sneezed again, bringing Dorothy's attention back to her mission.

"Let me know if you think of anything else," she said.

Artie nodded from behind his handkerchief and ended the video feed.

Dorothy pulled off her headset and leaned back in her chair. Solomon lifted his head from where he lay sleeping. He yawned and stretched and jumped from his chair to curl up in Dorothy's lap instead.

She absently stroked his fur, and Solomon reciprocated with a gentle purr. With Caprice gone, the next best agent for research was Sandi, a computer engineer in China who was a master at internet research. Then again, Destin had said there were no other agents available. That would have included Sandi. And Red.

The plane jerked, and Dorothy's heart pounded. She imagined one of the Dropa stones, or whatever they were, detaching from the plane and plummeting to the ground, followed closely by the plane itself. But the turbulence subsided, and Solomon continued to purr softly in her lap. She took several deep breaths, her mind drifting to thoughts of her father.

He had flown on this very plane and likely sat in the very seat Dorothy now occupied.

"Ms. Claes, I am afraid there are many things about Richard Van Damme that you do not know," Destin had said almost a year ago. Things everyone seemed bound and determined to keep Dorothy from ever knowing.

The snow continued to whip past the plane's windows. Solomon's purrs had become quieter as he fell asleep. Dorothy adjusted her legs, and he began purring again, stretching his toes wide.

"I won't stop," she whispered, more to herself than the cat. "I'll never stop."

She leaned into the armrest of the chair and stared out at the never-ending snow beyond.

THREE

"YES, I HAVE HIM. EVERYTHING'S ALL RIGHT, Aaron," Dorothy repeated for the fourth time.

Aaron had been trying to reach her for hours when he couldn't find Solomon in the apartment that morning. He had closed the shop and printed dozens of fliers to post around town. Luckily, Dorothy had returned his call before he had begun distributing them.

"He climbed inside my suitcase. Yes, I know. I don't know how customs didn't figure it out, either. I appreciate everything, Aaron. Take care."

The December wind whipped through Dorothy's long hair, making it feel colder than it truly was. The plane had landed smoothly at the Egilsstaðir airport, much to her relief. She held tight to the little cat and slipped her phone into her coat pocket as Artie carried her luggage to the rental car that waited for her. She followed close behind, trying to shield Solomon from the cold. She walked toward the rickety vehicle and opened her mouth to speak. This couldn't possibly be the car Destin had rented for her. The yellow VW donned several rust spots and a large tear in the headrest of the passenger seat. Dorothy cringed as she approached, taking in the scent of stale cigarettes and something that reminded her of cold French fries.

"Here," Artie said as she reached him. He held up a pair of shoelaces and blew his nose into his handkerchief. He wound one around Solomon, making a temporary harness and tying the second shoelace like a sort of leash. "At least until you can find something better," he said, stepping back and sneezing violently.

Dorothy looked down and saw Artie's lace-less shoes. She smiled and laid a hand on the man's arm. "You're wonderful, Artie. Thank you."

With another muffled sneeze, Artie put Dorothy's cat-free suitcase into the trunk of the little car as she climbed in. It had been years since she had driven a foreign vehicle, and Frank had done most of the driving. Solomon roamed the backseat before jumping into the back window. Artie closed the trunk and patted the roof of the little yellow VW.

"Stay safe, Fennec," he called through the window.

Dorothy nodded and eased her foot off the clutch. The car stalled. She glanced at Artie through the window, smiling apologetically.

"I got it – it's all right. Like riding a bicycle, right?"

She started the car again, easing off the clutch more slowly. The car jerked, and Solomon fell out of the back window, but the car remained in motion this time. Dorothy watched Artie in the review mirror as she shifted into second gear, and the little rental car zoomed away.

Iceland had been one of the last stops Dorothy and Frank had visited after she'd retired. Her friends raved about the hot springs, but the pair had found it too touristy for their tastes. Instead, they would sneak into the cruise ship docks of Reykjavík and chat with the strangers enjoying the fresh air and a smoke under the moonlight.

The wind whipped around the little car, which felt like a tin can on roller skates. Dorothy's grip tightened on the steering wheel as the mountain in the distance loomed ever closer. Despite the cold, Dorothy cracked her window, breathing in the crisp air. Solomon's nose twitched at the unfamiliar smells, and his pupils dilated as he watched the passing landscape from his resumed perch in the back window.

Dorothy rounded a corner, and a large sign greeted

her: *Welcome to Eskifjörður.*

She eased the little car down to first gear as she entered the heart of Eskifjörður. They passed little stone houses painted bright red, blue and purple. A towering apartment building sat far off the main road across from a maritime museum, long since closed.

Dorothy craned her neck, looking for her destination as Solomon meowed more and more with each passing mile. Finally, she spotted the Kaffihúsið Guesthouse and Bar & Grill and pulled the rickety car into the stone drive. Solomon bounded into the front seat, looking out the front windshield and continuing his meowing tirade.

"I'll find you a litter box as soon as I can," Dorothy said. She scratched the cat's ears, then hurried out of the vehicle before Solomon had a chance to dart out. She could hear his incessant and pathetic crying all the way to the front door.

The Kaffihúsið was smaller than Dorothy had expected. A tight staircase to her left led to the guestrooms above. To her right was the bar and grill of the Kaffihúsið, and to her utter embarrassment, it was packed with locals who gawked and stared as she approached the tiny check-in counter.

"Filip!" one of the locals called. "*Einhver er hérna.*"

A heavily bearded man emerged from the back of

the restaurant, wiping his hands on a white cloth and scratching at his apron strings. He smiled at Dorothy as he approached and pulled out a tiny pair of reading glasses.

"*Get ég hjálpað þér?*" he asked, opening the guestbook in front of him.

"Um," Dorothy stammered. Her mission to Paris had been easier since she knew a little French. Icelandic was a mystery to her. "I'm here to check in? Dorothy Fennec," she said uncertainly.

Filip flipped through the book before him as the chatter in the small restaurant started up again. Dorothy cast a nervous glance over her shoulder. She could see Solomon out the window, still meowing and pacing across the dashboard.

"Dorothy?" the man asked. "I have a Fanny Fennec."

Dorothy closed her eyes and sighed. "I prefer Dorothy, but yes, they probably made the registration under Fanny."

The man nodded, picking up a pencil to write something in his book.

Dorothy looked out the glass doors behind her. Solomon was now pawing at the windshield. "You wouldn't happen to have any place around here that I could get a litter box for my cat, would you?" she asked.

The man looked up, his eyes wide. *"Kotturinn þinn?"*

"He's very friendly!" Dorothy said, waving her hands in defense. "He... He climbed inside my suitcase."

Filip blinked at Dorothy for a moment, then started laughing. The noise in the restaurant dimmed slightly as several locals turned their attention to Dorothy once more.

"Ada!" the man called.

A blonde-haired girl pushed through the kitchen door, her brow furrowed in frustration.

"Já, hvað er það?" she asked.

"Will you call Margret and get her to bring some things for a cat?" Filip asked.

Ada's eyes widened as Filip's had, and she looked back and forth between the man and Dorothy.

"He's friendly," Dorothy repeated.

"He climbed inside her suitcase." Filip snickered.

Ada did not laugh. Instead, the look of worry deepened on her face.

"Is something wrong?" Dorothy asked. "He won't make a mess. He's traveled all over the world with me. I'll pay an extra security deposit."

Filip set a hand on Ada's shoulder and spoke quickly in Icelandic to her. Ada stormed off, but Filip turned back to Dorothy with a smile.

"Never mind, Ada," he said. "Come. You get the *köttur*. I will get your bags."

Dorothy led Filip toward the old, yellow car. He smiled when he saw Solomon sitting in the front seat, his paws on the steering wheel.

"He is ready to go!" Filip chuckled.

"Yes, hopefully not all over my rental," Dorothy murmured.

She opened the door and caught Solomon as he leapt out. She quickly heaved the struggling feline into her coat, zipping him up so only his head stuck out the top. "Now behave. You can explore when we get to our room."

Solomon mewed in protest as Dorothy followed Filip back into the building. Once the door had closed behind them, she released him from her coat, holding tight to the makeshift leash.

"Right this way," Filip said, leading the pair up the narrow staircase.

Solomon followed after the man, pulling Dorothy along by the shoestring leash. She tried to ignore the whispers and stares from the restaurant. They weren't the typical looks of awe and adoration she usually received when out with Solomon. Ada had quite perfectly expressed the feeling that lingered in the air around Solomon – fear.

Filip pushed open a door at the end of the hall. "Here you are," he said with a smile and nod.

"Thank you," said Dorothy as Solomon pushed past them and landed on the bed. She slipped off her coat and tossed it on the bed beside him. Solomon immediately pounced on it and buried his head in its folds.

"Oh!" Dorothy turned to Filip and saw him pointing at the little fox pin on her shirt. "You're here with Caprice," he said.

"You know Caprice?" Dorothy asked.

Filip nodded, and the same fear crept across the features of his previously happy face. "*Já*," he said, his eyes darting to where Solomon still played on the bed.

"Do you know where she is?" Dorothy asked, taking a step toward the man.

Footsteps in the hall beyond saved Filip from having to answer. He turned, and Dorothy saw Ada coming up behind him, two large bags in her hand. She handed them to Filip without a word, then hurried back down the tiny staircase.

"Is Ada all right?" Dorothy asked.

Filip handed the bags to Dorothy, the smile returning to his face. "Get your little *köttur* settled, then come down to the restaurant. My skyr-dogs are famous." He winked and closed the door behind him.

Dorothy sighed and turned back to Solomon, who looked at her innocently from beneath her coat.

"I don't care what Caprice said. You are not an honorary spy." She set the bag of cat supplies on the bed.

Solomon trilled and began his own investigation by sniffing the bags and the contents within.

Ten minutes and one of the largest bowel movements she had ever seen from a cat later, Dorothy attempted to leave her room. Solomon, however, refused to let her leave without him. She carefully tied Artie's shoelace-harness around the cat once more and scooped him into her outer cardigan.

When she reached the bottom step of the narrow stairwell, the locals had resumed their side glances. She stepped toward the edge of the restaurant area, lingering in the entrance and trying to catch someone's attention.

She saw Ada push her way out of the kitchen carrying a tray full of food. Dorothy smiled when the young woman caught her eye and waited patiently for her to deliver the food to a table.

"Can I help you?" Ada asked, keeping a moderate distance from Dorothy and eying the little black cat suspiciously.

"I-I was wondering if I could get some food for my

room. He doesn't want to let me out of his sight. The last time we were separated he – well…" Dorothy trailed off, hoping Ada wouldn't ask too many questions. She rubbed Solomon's ears absently, and the cat seemed to melt into her hand.

"Dorothy," came Filip's voice from across the room. "Here, sit," he said, gesturing toward a small table at the back of the room by one of the only windows.

Dorothy smiled at Ada, who frowned and stomped back to the kitchen. Night was beginning to fall, and a gentle dusting of snow had started to cover the ground and the little windowsill outside. Filip pulled the chair out for Dorothy, then disappeared into the kitchen again. Dorothy loosened her grip on Solomon and let him look out the window. She tried to ignore the whispers of the customers around her.

Why Destin had sent her, she had no idea. Caprice spoke Icelandic and would have been able to understand the conversations around her. Destin had said all other agents were deployed, which was also not typical since there was always at least one agent available to research.

Solomon turned from pouncing the snowflakes through the glass. His nostrils flared as Filip returned with a skyr-dog for Dorothy and a small bowl of fish for the little cat.

Dorothy looked at the plate before her. She had tried one of Iceland's famous hotdogs during her travels with Frank. Unlike an American hotdog, Iceland's were made from lamb, but she had never had skyr on a pylsur before. She dabbed at the condiment drizzled across the top and offered a lick to Solomon.

"Your *köttur* has good taste." Filip chuckled, taking the chair across from Dorothy.

"He should," she said. "He's traveled all over the world with me. We were in Paris only a year ago." Dorothy took a bite of the skyr-dog and felt her stomach grumble. Filip waited patiently for her to finish. He scratched Solomon's ears and was impressed the little cat knew how to give a high-five.

When Dorothy had finished, she pushed her plate toward Solomon and dabbed at her mouth with a napkin.

"What can you tell me about Caprice?" she asked bluntly. "I'm trying to find her. She hasn't been in contact with anyone for several days."

Filip stroked his beard and leaned across the table toward Dorothy.

"It got her too, I'm afraid," he said.

Dorothy leaned forward as well. "What got her?" Her heart began to pound, and she placed a protective hand on Solomon's back as the cat licked her plate clean.

Filip cleared his throat. "*Jólakötturinn*," he whispered. "The Yule cat."

A year ago, Dorothy wouldn't have believed there was any truth to myths and folklore. But if The Silver Foxes had taught her anything, it was never to dismiss a possible lead, no matter how farfetched it might seem.

"The Yule cat?" Dorothy asked. "But it's not Christmas yet."

Filip looked out into the crowd and lowered his voice more. "That is only scratching the surface, though. The true legends are more complicated than what most people care to believe. What do you know about *Jólakötturinn*?"

Dorothy bit her lip, trying to remember the tale she had learned many years ago.

"Just that the Yule cat eats naughty children who were not given new clothes for Christmas," she said shrugging.

Filip nodded.

"*Jólakötturinn* belongs to Gryla, the giantess. It is said she and her sons, the twelve Yule lads, live in this very mountain." He pointed out the dark window.

The Hólmatindur Mountain had been a near three-mile climb for Dorothy and Frank when they

38

visited Reykjavík during their travels. Their names were signed in its guestbook at the summit. But the Reykjavík side had been an easy climb in the middle of summer. She stared at the silhouette of the imposing mountain in the distance as Filip continued. He folded his hands on the table before him, rubbing his thumbs together.

"Emma was the first to go missing."

Dorothy sat straighter in her chair. "Who's Emma?"

"She was the first of our girls who were taken," Filip replied quietly, glancing around at the guests nearby.

"You mean it's not just Caprice? How many have there been?"

Filip scratched his beard. "Eight. Emma was taken on the twelfth, and Ava on the thirteenth."

Dorothy's heart quickened as Filip named off each young girl who had disappeared.

"You said they were taken. Who's taking them?"

"You need to understand," Filip said, "our unemployment rate has been on the rise for quite some time. We are a small fishing port, and we rely on tourism. But people cannot afford to travel to small towns like ours anymore. They need to experience as much as possible in one place, so they are staying in Reykjavík more and more. These families were not horrible to their children. They would have been given new clothes, but we did not know the warehouse was going to close."

Dorothy shook her head, realizing she probably should have taken a nap before trying to interview anyone for her mission. It was all so confusing.

"What warehouse?" she asked.

"The museum was being renovated into a warehouse, and many of the families here took up employment there. Two weeks ago, they showed up for work, and the doors were locked. No notice, no sign on the door."

"And all of the girls who have gone missing were employed there?"

Filip shook his head. "Their parents were. Hekla was only fifteen."

"Who took them? What does it have to do with Gryla and the Yule lads?"

Filip pulled at his beard again and shifted uncomfortably in his seat.

"It is the Yule cat, Dorothy. We think Gryla is sending her nasty beast to take our children. One of our daughters for each of her sons."

"And since these families can't afford Christmas presents, the Yule cat knows exactly who to target, right?" said a woman's voice over the din in the restaurant.

Dorothy and Filip looked up and saw a dark-haired woman step toward their table, a bottle of Garún in hand. She unceremoniously plunked herself in the chair by the window, and Dorothy pulled Solomon into her lap.

"Don't be like that, Hulda," said Filip.

"Like what? I cannot believe you all still accept these fairy tales. Our girls are missing, and you're just going to sit here and accept it like it is meant to be!"

"And how would you defy a giantess, Hulda?" a man from a neighboring table asked. "You think I can just walk into a cave and steal Ava back? You think I'm not trying to cooperate with the police? Do you have any idea how often I've prayed that she just ran off to Seyðisfjörður? *Megi tröll hafa þína vini.*"

Just before the dark-haired woman stood in protest, Solomon leapt from Dorothy's lap. He landed hard on the table, his fur raised along his spine. He hissed and growled at the woman, his eyes transfixed on something. Dorothy scooped him into her arms, trying to hush and calm the cat.

"Solomon, what's gotten into you?" she asked. "I'm so sorry. He's never like this. I don't know what's wrong."

Hulda glanced over her shoulder and seemed to go pale despite the alcoholic flush in her cheeks. She took one last look at Solomon, then left. The locals who had started to gather during her argument parted and stared after her.

"Thanks for dinner," Dorothy said to Filip. "If you could send Caprice's things to my room, I would appreciate it."

"Of course," Filip said, his voice strained.

Dorothy nodded her thanks and walked past the crowd toward her room, Solomon still growling in her arms.

FOUR

IT TOOK SEVERAL MINUTES FOR SOLOMON TO finally settle. He padded back and forth between the door and window, his tail puffed up and his pupils dilated. Dorothy laid her coat on the bed again, and Solomon snuggled beneath it. Once he was no longer growling and his fur lay flat, Dorothy took a long, hot shower.

She was grateful for the soothing steam that billowed around her, and thankful Iceland's water was naturally heated geothermally. She could almost feel her joints loosen as she stood beneath the narrow stream of water. She closed her eyes and let her thoughts wander.

She hadn't had time to brush up on Icelandic folklore. That was, of course, Caprice's specialty. She was not only fluent in the lore of her own country of

South Africa, but her knowledge of myth and folklore throughout the world was unsurpassed by anyone Dorothy had yet met.

What she *had* remembered from her travels with Frank was how much the Icelanders believed their myths and legends to be true. To them, fey and trolls were as real as the sheep grazing in their pastures. Which meant it would be more difficult for Dorothy to ask if anything odd had recently happened.

Dorothy stepped from the shower and found Solomon had opened the bathroom door. He wound around her legs, purring and licking the water from her feet as she sat on the edge of the bed. She squeezed her hair between the towel and stared out the window before her.

The sun had completely set, and she could see tiny lights dotted across the dark landscape. Solomon pressed his paws against the glass and huffed. He turned and ran to the door, sniffing at the space beneath it. Dorothy knew someone was there before she heard the knock.

"Just a moment!" she called, hurriedly pulling on her nightdress.

She picked up Solomon and opened the door. Ada stood in the hall, a heavy bag slung over her shoulder and a suitcase trailing behind her.

"Filip said to bring these to you," she said, casting a nervous glance at Solomon. Dorothy opened the door for her, and Ada set Caprice's belongings inside.

"Her account has already been paid," Ada said before carefully stepping back into the hall. "Do you need anything else?"

"No. Thank you, Ada," Dorothy said.

The young woman turned on her heel and headed down the hall before Dorothy had closed the door.

Solomon immediately jumped from her arms and began rubbing against Caprice's suitcase. He pawed at the zippers, which jingled and made him pounce on the bag, knocking it over.

"Leave it," Dorothy said, stuffing the suitcase beneath the bed with her own.

She hoisted the bag onto her bed and began emptying its contents. She pulled out a stack of folders, each containing the name of one of the missing girls. She opened the first folder.

Emma Hafnarsdottir – December 12th

A picture fell out of the stack of paperwork inside. The bright, smiling face of a teenage girl stared up at her. She couldn't have been more than seventeen years old.

Dorothy sighed and set the papers aside. This wasn't

just about Caprice anymore. Eight girls had gone missing. Despite what she told herself about staying in The Silver Foxes to learn the truth about her father's death, *this* was the real reason she stayed.

She opened the files again. Each file detailed the girls' families. Who their parents were, their siblings, and how and what jobs they all had held at the warehouse. Dorothy rummaged through the bag once more and pulled out a spiral notebook. Caprice had scribbled several notes across it, mostly in Icelandic.

Jólasveinarnir

Jólakötturinn

Dorothy turned the page and saw another name scrawled in hurried handwriting.

Hulda Svanursdottir

Solomon bounded from beneath the bed toward the door again with an excited trill. He stood on his hind legs and began pawing at the door knob. Dorothy caught him just in time as the door popped open.

The dark-haired woman from the restaurant stood outside, a look of surprise on her face. Dorothy's face must have looked equally surprised. She looked from the woman to the struggling cat in her arms. He showed no aggression toward her like he had earlier.

"I –" Hulda began, her rolling Icelandic accent catching in her throat. "I did not mean to disturb you."

"Not at all," Dorothy said and held tighter to Solomon, who seemed determined to investigate the woman.

"I wanted to apologize," she said as she motioned toward Solomon. "I did not mean to upset your cat."

Solomon finally wiggled free and leapt to the floor, winding himself around the woman's ankles and purring. She bent to pet him, and Solomon graciously accepted. Dorothy only stared.

"What's his name?" the woman asked.

"Uh – Solomon," Dorothy stammered.

A smiled curled at the woman's lips. "He certainly is a little king."

Solomon bounded back to Dorothy, and she scooped him up again.

"Well, he doesn't seem to hold a grudge, so neither do I." Dorothy held out a hand, and the dark-haired woman shook it. "I'm Dorothy."

"Hulda," the woman said with a smile.

Dorothy cleared her throat, her mind flashing back to Caprice's list.

"I heard he climbed into your suitcase?"

Dorothy sighed. "Yes. I was packing in a hurry. He must have snuck in when I wasn't looking."

Hulda chuckled. "Are you here visiting family? Most travelers don't come until it is warmer."

A gust of wind shook the window behind Dorothy as if on cue. "Business, actually. I own an antique shop in the States."

Hulda nodded and fiddled anxiously with something in her pocket. "I suppose many of the families here will be getting rid of some of their belongings. They're relocating now that the warehouse is closed. And what with the…" She trailed off, squeezing whatever was in her pocket tight in her hand.

"I'm sure there's an explanation," Dorothy said, setting a consoling hand on Hulda's arm.

She nodded and swallowed. "There is. And it's *not* the trolls, no matter what anyone says."

Dorothy tilted her head. "You don't believe what everyone's saying?"

Hulda scoffed. "That the Yule lads are using their mother's giant cat to steal little girls to be their brides? No. It is ridiculous."

"What *do* you think it is?"

Hulda pulled the object from her pocket and squeezed it tighter. "Something far more human. At least I hope so." She was silent for several moments, and Dorothy saw her pocket the object again. "Well, as I said, I wanted to apologize for upsetting Solomon.

I will not keep you. *Góða nótt.*"

She turned as quickly as Ada had and disappeared down the tiny staircase.

Dorothy closed her door for what she hoped was the last time that night and deposited Solomon on the bed. He meowed curtly at his human, then began kneading on Dorothy's coat again .

Dorothy sat on the edge of the bed and sighed. Caprice's mission folders still lay strewn across the bed behind her. She picked them up and placed them carefully in her fellow agent's bag before climbing under the covers and pulling out her cell phone. Dorothy knew Red was likely to be knee-deep in his own mission, but she needed to hear a familiar voice.

She dialed his number, and Red's cheerful voice answered immediately.

"How's my favorite foxy lady?" he asked with a chuckle.

Dorothy smiled. "Do you want a cat?"

Red paused. Dorothy imagined him squinting in confusion. "Do I want a cat?"

"You won't believe what Solomon did."

"Oh, I might." Red laughed. Dorothy heard what sounded like street music in the background.

"Where are you?" she asked.

"On assignment. Did you know there was an actual

THE SILVER FOX MYSTERIES

case of people dancing themselves to death in the 1500s? Apparently, it's back. Or something like it."

"I would have thought Jorge would have taken that assignment, what with being a professional dancer."

"It seems Destin has us all running ragged right now. But tell me, what did my favorite little panther get into this time?"

Dorothy pulled the covers up around her, and Solomon settled innocently into the crook of her arm, purring and rubbing on the hand that held her phone.

"He climbed into my suitcase. I didn't realize it until I was at the airport. There wasn't time to take him back because of the storm. Did you know Artie is allergic to cats?"

"Artie's allergic to everything," Red said, laughing.

Dorothy's smile deepened, and she felt her heart lighten.

"So, Solomon's on mission with you again then?" Red asked after his laughter had died away.

"It's not like Paris. He'll have to stay in my room, though he's going to hate it," said Dorothy.

"Take him with you! Who doesn't love a cat walking on a leash?"

"Apparently, the people here." Dorothy sighed again and scratched Solomon behind his ears. "They think a – a giant, mythological cat is behind what's going on. So, a stranger showing up with a cat hasn't been very well received."

She wanted to tell him more. She wanted to tell him all about the missing girls and how the responsibility of their return weighed on her . She wanted more than anything to feel his calloused hands reach for hers and reassure her that everything was going to work out. But for everyone's safety, the foxes were not permitted to speak of their missions to each other.

"They just need a chance to get to know him. You know I wasn't much of a cat person when we met. Now I love the little guy."

Solomon chirped and rubbed on the phone again, making Red chuckle.

"I just don't know if I trust him right now. You wouldn't believe what he did, Red. He almost attacked someone."

"Solomon did that?"

"He did. This woman, she sat at our table and he started growling and hissing at her out of nowhere."

"That doesn't sound like him," Red said, his voice now full of concern.

"No, it definitely does not. But what's even stranger is she came to apologize just a few minutes ago, and he was perfectly fine with her."

"Could be the smell," Red said. "Cats have a

stronger sense of smell than dogs. Maybe he got a whiff of something that wasn't related to the woman at all. Animals also see on a different spectrum than us. He might have seen something too."

"I guess," Dorothy mused. "She was sitting by a window. A breeze could have blown something in, or maybe he saw something to do with the artifact."

"See? I bet it was nothing. You do what you think is best, but I think that cat of yours has some instincts that could be used to your advantage on this case."

"You might be right."

"'Course I am! Now, when are you coming back to the ranch? I have a candlelit dinner in the barn with your name on it. It's not Paris, but I promise the food's delicious."

"We'll have to set up a table for Solomon and Ruby then, seeing as how he likes to invite himself along to things."

"That can definitely be arranged."

Dorothy and Red chatted well into the night until the woman's eyelids began to droop and Solomon had long since fallen asleep. They finally said their good-byes, and Dorothy ended the call with a heavy sigh.

She reached for her charging cable, trying not to disturb the little cat when her suitcase began to buzz. She almost dropped her phone in her haste to answer

Destin's call.

She swiped at the green button, and Destin's face appeared.

"Fennec," he said.

"Hello, Destin."

"Have you found anything?" His voice was strained, and his typical smoothed-back hair looked messy.

"Destin, I only just got here."

Destin turned to look at something to his left, then turned back to the screen. "I suppose you're right. I must have been looking at the wrong clock. Have you found any leads?"

"I'm not sure. The locals here seem to think it's the Icelandic Christmas cat. Everyone seems to have some connection to a warehouse here as well."

"A warehouse? What do you know about it? Have you explored it yet?"

"Destin," Dorothy said warningly.

The man held up a hand. "Sorry. I know."

"It seems one day, the warehouse just closed. People showed up for work, but the place was locked. That's when the disappearances started."

"Yes, the children," Destin said nonchalantly.

"Could you look into it for me?" Dorothy asked.

"Look into it?"

"The Warehouse. Maybe find out who the business

owner or manager was. There has to be someone more I can talk to."

Destin ran a hand over his hair, but it bounced back. He sighed and turned to his left again. "I need to check in with Kitty. I'll see what I can find, Fennec. Just find Caprice and get out of there."

The screen turned black, and Destin was gone. Solomon yawned and stretched, his back feet pushing into the small of Dorothy's back. She ignored him. Something about Destin was off, but she couldn't put her finger on it. She tucked the tablet back into her suitcase, shoved Solomon over, and crawled back beneath the covers.

FIVE

DOROTHY WAS SURE FILIP OR ADA WERE GOING to withdraw her reservation and ask her to leave. She could hear Solomon through the second-story window as she walked down to the general store to buy him more cat food. When she returned, he had somehow climbed the curtain and was precariously balancing on the rod.

He leapt to the floor before she had set down the bag and began winding himself around her ankles, as though he hadn't seen her in months.

"There's no way you're going to let me leave you here, are you?" she asked as Solomon wolfed down his food. She sighed and pulled out a new leash and harness from the bag. It wasn't the vest-style the little cat was used to, but Solomon would just have to deal with it.

After he had thoroughly cleaned his face and paws,

Dorothy slipped the harness over him and let him run around the room while she ate the breakfast Filip delivered upon her return.

Caprice would have known about the lore of the Yule cat. That's why Destin had sent her on this mission in the first place. If Dorothy were going to start somewhere, it would have to be with the Yule cat.

Solomon leapt on the bed, stepping on the bag of food and treats. Dorothy picked him up and clipped the leash to his harness.

"Come on," she said as she reached for her purse. "Maybe we can burn off some of your energy."

They descended the narrow staircase, Solomon leading the way with his tail held high. Filip was in the restaurant wiping down the last of the tables from the breakfast rush.

"Filip?" Dorothy called to him.

The man smiled beneath his beard. He draped the damp cloth over the back of a chair and sauntered toward the pair.

"Heading out for some sightseeing?" he asked. "There is not much around here these days."

"Do you have a library?" she asked. "I want to know more about this Yule cat."

Filip furrowed his brow and scratched at the apron strings tied around his waist. "*Bókasafn*? We have never had a library here, but I think Ada might be able to help you."

This time, Dorothy's brow furrowed. "Ada?"

Filip nodded. "She has the largest collection of books in town. Bit of a hoarder, if you ask me."

"Are you sure?" Dorothy looked at Solomon, who was sniffing at the legs of the check-in stand. "I-I hate to be a bother about it, but I'm not sure she trusts me very much."

Filip laughed. "Ada does not trust anyone. It's why I hired her, to be honest. She keeps a watchful eye on the tourists. Never mind her. I will give her a ring and let her know you are on your way. We're not scheduled to have any guests arrive today, and the restaurant does not open until later."

"If you're sure," Dorothy said.

"If reading and research is what you need, then Ada is your girl." He reached behind the check-in stand and pulled out an old corded phone.

After what sounded like quite the argument in Icelandic on Ada's part, Filip hung up the phone. He wrote down an address and handed it to Dorothy.

"Ada lives in the apartments as you are entering town. This is her address. She is expecting you, and I have told her to be nice."

Dorothy accepted the piece of paper before Solomon

could jump and knock it from the man's hand.

"Thank you," she said. She wound Solomon's leash more securely around her hand, and, clicking her tongue at the little cat, headed for the door.

The winters in Iceland were plenty cold, but it was nothing compared to the arctic winds that had been blasting Lexington, Massachusetts for the last few weeks. This was what winter was supposed to feel like. Solomon bounded in the snowbanks ahead of Dorothy as the pair walked along the bustling street. She recognized several of the people from the restaurant the night before. They walked or drove up and down the street, hung signs in the windows of their little shops or stopped to pet Solomon as they went.

Dorothy had to admit, the cat was a great ice breaker. It was only when he tired of walking, and Dorothy was sequestered to being his personal valet, did she question whether she should have left him back at the Kaffihúsið.

It was a good twenty-minute hike to Ada's apartment building. It was plain-looking, with tiny windows and a large, gravel parking area. Dorothy set Solomon down once they were in the warmth of the building, and he bounded up the stairs before her, stopping only when he felt the tug from nearly pulling Dorothy's arm off.

By the time they reached the third floor, Dorothy's knees were beginning to crack and pop. She paused, rubbing a hand over her knee and elbow as Solomon spun in circles, his cheerful and excited chatter echoing through the halls.

A door opened, and both Solomon and Dorothy jumped. The head and shoulders of a blonde-haired young woman peeked into the hall.

"I thought I heard a cat," came Ada's voice. Dorothy scooped Solomon into her arms and headed up the hall.

"Hello, Ada," she said, holding out a hand to the young woman. "Thank you for helping me."

Ada shook Dorothy's hand and dropped it quickly. She held the door open and allowed Dorothy to enter.

Filip had not been wrong. Every wall was lined with bookcases filled with books. Everything from graphic novels to old copies of *The Encyclopedia Britannica*. They stepped farther into the little living room, and Dorothy saw a shelf in the kitchen lined with at least a dozen cooking books.

"Filip said you want to know more about *Jólaköttur*."

"The what?" Dorothy asked. She still hadn't quite figured out the rolling Icelandic dialect, and it was difficult to know whether someone was speaking Icelandic or English to her at times.

Ada rolled her eyes. "The Yule cat," she said slowly.

"Oh." Dorothy blushed and set Solomon on the floor at her feet. "If it'll help me find my friend, then yes."

"Follow me," Ada said. She led the way down a tiny hall and opened one of the doors. Inside were more bookcases and at least twenty boxes stacked precariously on the floor and on the edge of a desk.

Ada flipped on the light and headed for the tower of boxes. Dorothy watched as she opened a box, dug through the piles of books inside, then set the box aside and reached for another.

Solomon threatened to scale the bookcase as Ada worked, but Dorothy held him back. Instead, he paced as far as his leash would allow, calling into the corners of the room to hear his voice echo like he used to do as a kitten.

"Hush," Dorothy said.

"You can let him go if you want," Ada said, surprising Dorothy.

"I like cats. I doubt he'll hurt anything. I have all my rare books in my bedroom anyway."

"Are you sure?" Dorothy asked.

Ada looked up, her blonde hair clinging to the sweat on her forehead. "*Já*. I wouldn't have suggested it if I weren't sure. Besides, if it gets him to stop meowing…" She returned to the box of books, not bothering to wipe the hair from her face.

Dorothy shrugged and unhooked Solomon's leash. In an instant, he had climbed onto the desk and shoved his head into the box with Ada. He seemed to scrutinize each book she pulled from its depths as much as the young woman did.

Finally, Ada heaved one of the largest boxes onto the desk. She opened it and wiped away a layer of dust.

"I know it has to be in this room," she said. "It's been a while since I wrote my thesis, but I saved every book."

"Oh?" Dorothy asked, attempting to break the awkward tension that hung in the air. "What was it about?"

"How the economy of Iceland is affected by our myths and legends," she said matter-of-factly. "My professor was not impressed. She failed me."

"What did you study?" Dorothy asked, taking a step toward one of the bookshelves and looking at the label taped to the side. Ada had organized her books using the Dewey Decimal System, and Dorothy smiled.

"Literature," she said. "Ah, here it is." She pulled what looked like an old children's book from the box and wiped a layer of dust from the cover. "My *au pair* bought this for me to help me learn English," she said. "It has Icelandic on one page and the English translation on the other." She handed the book to Dorothy and gave Solomon a short pet before closing up the box.

"You can give it to Filip when you're finished with it."

"Thank you," Dorothy said.

Ada nodded and led the way out of the room. Solomon ran ahead of her, and Dorothy quickly followed, praying the cat didn't knock anything over. There were towers of books and boxes – which Dorothy now assumed contained more books – stacked everywhere.

"If there's nothing else you need, I have some reviews I have to finish filming." Ada gestured toward a camera that sat on an end table Dorothy had previously overlooked.

"You film reviews? Of books?" Dorothy asked.

Ada nodded. "And I upload them to the internet. I have a pretty big following. But I lost some time when the girls went missing. Everyone was out looking for them the first few nights. But Reykjavík sent over that detective, and most of us have backed off. Except for the families, of course."

Dorothy nodded. "I'm sure it can't be easy."

Ada nodded and nonchalantly scratched Solomon where he stood on the back of her armchair.

"If you want to look me up, here's my website. I should have this video up by tonight. Might give you something to do." She handed Dorothy a business card and turned her attention back to Solomon.

"Thank you, Ada. You have no idea how much I appreciate this."

Ada nodded again, her mouth remaining in a thin, pressed line.

Dorothy clipped Solomon's leash to his harness, and the cat headed straight for the door.

"He knows what he's doing, *já*," Ada said as she held the door open for Dorothy.

"I don't know what he knows, but sometimes I think it's more than I know."

For the first time, Dorothy saw Ada grin.

"Good luck, Dorothy," she said before closing the door behind the pair.

With Ada's book tucked beneath her arm, Dorothy headed back to her room at the Kaffihúsið. They hadn't been at Ada's long, but with the sun higher in the sky, it wasn't as bitterly cold of a walk. This time, Solomon didn't demand to be held, which was a relief to Dorothy, as Ada's book was not a small one.

She opened the door to the bed and breakfast just in time to hear Filip's voice shouting from the kitchen.

Dorothy and Solomon both paused. The cat's ears

pricked forward, and Dorothy felt her hand slide into her purse, her fingers curling around her Smith & Wesson.

"Það er allt eyðilagt! Sérhver gámur skyr! Hvað eigum við að gera?"

The kitchen door slammed open, and Filip stormed out, his face bright red against the white of his apron.

"Is everything all right?" Dorothy asked, her hand still touching the gun in her purse.

Filip started when he saw her. He stopped and took a deep breath, scratching at the apron strings more violently this time.

"All our skyr has soured," he seethed. "I told Kristofer to set out a bowl last night. Cursed Skyrgámur."

"Sorry?" Dorothy asked as Solomon leapt onto the check-in stand and pawed at the air before Filip.

"One of *Jólasveinarnir*. Though if it saves one of the girls, I would rather they sour the skyr than take another bride."

Solomon gave an inquisitive mew, and Filip smiled, reaching down to pet the little cat's ears.

"So, you're saying a bowl of skyr would have warded off this Skyrgámur?" Dorothy asked.

"Not warded off, but it was an offering of sorts. *Bölvaður asninn!* That skyr is vital to many of our recipes."

Filip sighed and patted Solomon's back.

"If there's anything I can do to help," Dorothy began, but Filip held up his hand.

"*Þakka þér*, Dorothy, but you focus on finding your friend. We'll figure out another dish for tonight. Was Ada able to help you?" He gestured toward the book in Dorothy's hand.

"Oh, yes. At least I hope so."

"Well, if it's not what you are looking for, I am sure she has more." Filip raised his eyebrows and Dorothy chuckled.

"You weren't kidding about her collection."

Filip whispered "*hoarder*" under his breath and headed back toward the kitchen, his face returning to a normal color.

Dorothy looked at Solomon, who gave a single, pitiful meow, his paw still raised in the air.

"Sounds like there won't be any skyr-dogs tonight, little one," she said.

Solomon huffed. He flicked his paw and jumped down from the check-in stand. He gave a long, forlorn look over his shoulder toward the restaurant and the door Filip had disappeared through before heading up the narrow staircase with Dorothy.

As a child, Dorothy had been an avid reader. She had treasured the books she had owned and lovingly cared for the ones she'd checked out from her local library. She had hoped to one day share the experience with children of her own. On stormy nights, when she'd been curled up in bed with her books, Frank snoring quietly beside her, she'd dreamed of the snuggles and giggles she would share over a mug of hot chocolate as she read her favorite tales to her sons or daughters.

Those dreams had never come to be, but that had never stopped Dorothy and Frank from doting on Mary Pat's children and grandchildren.

As Dorothy kicked off her shoes and laid her coat on the end of the bed for Solomon to snuggle into, the fleeting memories of hot chocolate and giggles with her nephew, Craig, came back to her. She sighed and opened the book Ada had given her as Solomon batted at her toes.

The Christmas Cat of Iceland by Jóhannes úr Kötlum.

The book was older than Dorothy had first thought. It must have once belonged to Ada's *au pair*. The binding creaked as she opened it, and the familiar smell from her past met her nose. Solomon peeked from beneath her coat, sniffing the air.

"'You all know the Yule cat, and the cat was huge indeed,'" Dorothy read aloud. Solomon kneaded the comforter, listening to every word Dorothy spoke. The poem was long, and Dorothy found the English translations to be harsh and clumsy. When she finished, Solomon mewed from beneath her coat, his tail sticking out through the collar and thrashing back and forth.

She closed the book, reaching beneath the covers toward the little cat.

"Are you a ferocious kitty?" she asked, citing a line for the poem.

Solomon responded by pouncing on her hands beneath the blanket. Dorothy wiggled her fingers, and again the cat pounced. As suddenly as he had started playing, Solomon stopped. He popped out of the coat and bounded toward the window.

Dorothy heard the commotion a moment later. She joined Solomon at the window, peering down at the street below. Three large vans came to a screeching stop in the middle of the main road. The first two vans reversed, positioning themselves with their back doors thrown wide for the entire town center to see. From the third van, what looked like a TV reporter jumped out the front seat, followed closely by a cameraman.

They hurried toward the back of the first two vans as the shopkeepers emerged from the stores.

Dorothy headed for the door, Solomon on her heels.

"Not this time, little one," she said, pushing him back into the room and hurrying down the tiny staircase.

When she reached the bottom, she nearly crashed into Filip.

"What's going on?" Dorothy asked.

"Reporters," Filip seethed and mumbled what Dorothy was sure was a string of Icelandic curses and swears.

She watched as Filip stormed out the front door. She could now see the first two vans were loaded down with boxes of clothes. The cameraman counted down the reporter, whose worried face flew into an expression of glee in an instant.

The people in the back of the vans sprang into action. They began unloading boxes right onto the street as the reporter yammered away in Icelandic.

A man who had emerged from the hardware store across the street crept slowly closer. The reporter must have spotted him, as he suddenly ran to the man, brandishing the microphone in his face.

The man took a step back, holding the bags he carried with a white-knuckled grasp. He tried to push the reporter away, but the reporter followed on the man's heels.

Dorothy gasped when he stepped away from the shadows of the building. It was the man from the restaurant the night before. Ava's father. He turned again when the reporter refused to relent, his face a bright red. Dorothy didn't think his grip could get any tighter on the bags, and she worried what else he might do with his clenched fists.

Filip ran into the street, forcing his way between the man and the reporter. But it was too late. A shouting match had ensued.

The feeling in Dorothy's stomach tightened. This wasn't right. She pushed the door open, ready to step up to the defense of the families as well. Her feet carried her across the gravel parking lot, past her little yellow VW. Before she stepped onto the pavement of the road, a figure blocked her path.

"Stay here." It was Hulda.

Dorothy halted, watching as she ran headlong into the shouting match.

This time, the reporter turned his sights on Hulda. The camera flipped around, and the microphone was thrust into her face. She didn't shout or try to push it away. She stood straight, looking directly into the camera.

Dorothy watched as Hulda reached into her coat pocket. Dorothy pushed the door open, watching intently. Hulda flashed whatever was in her hand at the reporters, and their moods immediately changed. Could this be the artifact? An artifact that made people do whatever you wanted? Dorothy fought the urge to run headlong into the street and rip the object from Hulda's hands.

Filip and several other people took the reporters' distraction as an opportunity to lead Ava's father away and into the safety of the Kaffihúsið. Dorothy watched as they passed by, but her eyes were transfixed on Hulda. What Dorothy wouldn't give for another Karlee at that moment – someone who could translate for her and tell her what was being said.

She held the door open for Filip, Ava's father, and two other men who had joined them. They ushered the man to the restaurant, and Filip ran to the back, returning quickly with a bottle of beer.

"Is he all right?" Dorothy whispered to Filip as he came to stand beside her. They stared out the window at the reporter and his assistants as they loaded the clothes back into the van, Hulda watching over them.

Filip shook his head. "He is madder than a sinner on Sunday."

"What happened?" Dorothy asked.

"A bunch of *fífl* got together and thought if they donated clothes to us it would protect the children. They do not mean it. It is a joke to them."

Dorothy stared out the window in silence, watching as the reporter shouted at the people packing up the clothes.

Craig had developed a superstition after falling out of a tree as a child and breaking his arm in three places. Any time anyone used the phrase *knock on wood*, Craig would search feverishly for something wooden to knock on three times. It became a running joke in the family to use the phrase just to tease the poor boy.

It was easy to scoff and laugh at people who believed in the power of such things. It was another matter entirely when you were the one believing it.

The man in the restaurant finished his beer and rose from his chair.

"*Þakka þér fyrir,*" he said as he headed for the door. He paused when he saw Dorothy, looking at her from head to toe.

"You are the American with the cat," he said, his accent so heavy, Dorothy barely understood.

"Yes," Dorothy answered. "He won't hurt anyone."

"My daughter loved cats," he said. "She wanted one for Christmas every year since she was three." He seemed to look straight through Dorothy, lost in distant memory.

Without another word, he turned toward the door, watching as the vans sped away up the street, and headed out into the cold, December air.

SIX

DOROTHY HEARD SOLOMON BEFORE SHE SAW him. He must have known she was coming because he began his pitiful meowing as soon as she reached the top stair. He tried to shove his paws underneath the door but was only successful in smooshing himself against the frame.

She opened the door carefully, pushing the cat aside. Solomon rolled over and immediately leapt into the woman's arms. She caught him mid-jump, and he pushed hard into the side of her neck.

"I was barely gone twenty minutes," she said, scratching beneath his chin and sitting on the bed. With her single free hand, she pulled out the files from Caprice's bag again.

In the restaurant the night before, Filip had told her Ava had been taken on the thirteenth. Dorothy flipped through the paperwork until she found the paper for Ava. The girl's father had been employed to renovate the warehouse. She set Solomon on the bed beside her and sifted through the other files.

Solomon pounced at Caprice's bag, sending a cascade of files and notebooks to the floor.

"Solo –" Dorothy stopped. A tiny notebook that she had previously missed landed on top of the pile. She reached for it as Solomon climbed inside the now-empty bag.

December 12 – Emma, 16

December 13 – Ava, 15

December 14 – Elsabet, 8

December 15 – Maja, 10

December 16 – Silfa, 15

December 17 –

It had now been four days since Caprice had disappeared, and more girls had gone missing in the meantime.

Solomon poked his head out of Caprice's bag, and Dorothy squinted at him, thinking.

"Maybe you can help me after all, little one," she said and shoved the notebook into her pocket.

Solomon crawled out of the bag and stretched across the woman's lap, exposing his belly for tummy tickles.

Dorothy obliged with a smile. "Exactly," she said.

She slipped on his harness and leash once more and headed down the narrow staircase. She could hear Filip's voice before she reached the bottom. He spoke quickly into the corded phone behind the check-in desk. Dorothy waited patiently for him, but Solomon paced back and forth, mewing at both Filip and Dorothy.

When he finally hung up the phone, he didn't seem to notice Dorothy. He scratched at his apron strings with one hand and pulled at his beard with the other, looking into the empty restaurant space.

"Filip?" Dorothy asked.

Filip jumped and turned toward her. "Dorothy!" he said. "You gave me a fright."

"I'm sorry. Is everything all right?"

Filip looked over his shoulder at the restaurant again and sighed. "I should not be telling you this, but since you are staying here, you'll find out soon enough."

Solomon meowed at the man and placed a paw on his leg. Filip smiled and bent to pet the little cat.

"That was Detective Svanursdottir. She has a plan for protecting the rest of the children."

"And she called *you*?"

Filip nodded. "The Kaffihúsið has the largest open area in town short of hunkering down in the hay of someone's barn. She wants all the children to stay here tonight. So, looks like I will be clearing out the tables and chairs instead of working on that new recipe."

Dorothy reached into her pocket and pulled out Caprice's tiny notebook.

"Filip, I need your help," she said. "I need to know who the other girls are. There might be a connection the detectives haven't found yet that can lead me to Caprice."

She held out the notebook and pen to him. Solomon still sat at his feet, one paw on the man's shoe. He mewed pitifully up at him. Filip frowned. He pulled at his beard and glanced at the front door nervously.

"Detective Svanursdottir is not investigating your friend," he said. "I suppose if you do not find her, who will?"

He took the notebook from Dorothy and filled in the missing girls' names and ages, along with the dates they'd disappeared. He handed it back to Dorothy and stooped to pet Solomon again.

"Thank you, Filip," Dorothy said, tucking the notebook in her pocket. "I thought a visit from Solomon might cheer the families up."

She scooped Solomon into her arms, flashing a

75

reassuring smile at the man. "Ava's father seemed pretty upset by that incident earlier."

"Viktor," Filip said, nodding in agreement. "He has two more children. I cannot imagine..." He turned, looking at Dorothy for the first time in several moments. He sighed and smiled. "They are a good three miles north of here. It is a bright blue barn. You can't miss it."

Dorothy nodded and set a hand on Filip's shoulder.

"Thank you," she said again and headed toward her rental car.

The road turned to gravel just outside the town limits, and then to dirt shortly after that. The puddles that dotted the road were covered in a thin sheet of ice that snapped under the weight of the flimsy car. Solomon didn't seem to mind the bouncing now that his bladder had been relieved , unlike the ride into town night before. Dorothy, on the other hand, could feel her joints creaking and crunching with each dip and jerk of the car.

They crested a hill and the sight of a bright blue barn greeted them. Dorothy pulled into the drive and parked beside a moving van that was already half loaded down.

She gathered Solomon into her arms and headed toward the front door. A bouncing little girl, no more than fourteen, skipped down the front steps. The box in her hands overflowed with blankets and a small, stuffed penguin. She skidded to a stop when she saw Dorothy.

"Hello," Dorothy said. "Are your parents here? I thought you might like a visit from –"

A stern looking man stepped into the doorway. "Isabelle," he said. "*Komdu inn.*"

The girl hurried back up the steps, the penguin threatening to bounce out of the box.

"Can I help you?" the man asked in English, stepping down the stairs and eyeing both Dorothy and Solomon with suspicion.

"You must be Viktor," said Dorothy, holding out a hand to the man. "I'm Dorothy, and this is Solomon."

Viktor took a tentative step forward. He barely touched Dorothy's hand before dropping it again.

"I heard about Ava," Dorothy said, and the man stiffened. "I thought you might like a visit from Solomon."

"I do not think this is a good idea," he said. "I can not risk my other children."

"Solomon isn't the Yule cat," Dorothy said, setting the cat at her feet. He immediately began sniffing the puddle that stood between his human and the man. "He was rescued from Tibet six years ago. My husband found him. He's traveled all over the world with us. He was even in a cat show in Paris last year."

Viktor seemed to relax as he watched Solomon bat at the water.

"I appreciate that you want to help, but now is not a good time." He nodded toward the moving truck. "We are moving in with my brother."

"What about Ava?" Dorothy asked.

Viktor swallowed. "I am not leaving her, if that is what you think. But I have two other girls I must protect. I never should have taken that job."

"At the warehouse?"

Viktor nodded. "Most of the renovations had been done, and they were starting to receive inventory. I worked at the shipping docks."

"What was the inventory?" Dorothy watched as Solomon's ears pricked up and he turned toward the side of the house. She tightened her grip on the end of his leash.

The man shrugged. "Mostly just –"

An ear-piercing scream ripped through the air. Solomon tore after the sound, pulling the leash from Dorothy's hand.

"Solomon!" she screamed.

"Isabelle!" Viktor cried, and the pair ran after Solomon to the back of the house.

The cat stood in the middle of the yard, his fur fluffed from nose to tail. The remnants of what looked like a snowman stood to one side. He stared across the barren landscape, still hissing and pawing at a large chunk of black fur in his mouth.

"Solomon, it's all right," Dorothy said, carefully reaching out a hand to him. He growled and spun as soon as he felt her touch. He raised a paw, then lowered it again when he saw who it was.

"Isabelle!" A large woman ran out the back door, a baby on her hip.

Dorothy quickly scooped up Solomon and pulled the chunk of fur from his mouth. The hairs were much longer and thicker than his. She shoved the hair into the pocket of her coat and turned to the frantic family beside her.

"*Hvar er Isabelle?*" Viktor asked the woman.

"*Ég hélt að hún væri með þér,*" the woman replied, her voice tight with fear.

"*Ég sagði henni að fara aftur inni,*" he replied.

"We need to call the police," Dorothy said.

"Who are you?" the woman demanded, her voice near shrieking.

"*Hún er rétt,* Sara," Viktor said.

Sara's breathing was fast and heavy. Her lip began to tremble as she ran back inside the house.

Solomon was clutching Dorothy's shoulder, all his claws digging into her coat. She could feel him trembling as he continued to stare across the empty pasture. She reached into her pocket and pulled out her cell phone. She took several pictures of the trampled snow, the snowman, and where Solomon kept staring. The man took off toward the barn, calling desperately for his daughter.

Dorothy almost overlooked it at first. A single, large pawprint was stamped into the snow by the destroyed snowman. It was huge, almost the size of a bear's paw.

Dorothy leaned down as best she could, Solomon still clinging to her shoulder. She studied the area carefully, but there were no other prints leading to or away from the scene.

Dorothy's heart raced. The girl had been snatched seemingly out of thin air. There were no footprints, save for the ones by the snowman and Solomon's tiny pawprints. She could hear the woman, Sara, sobbing from inside the house. She wanted to comfort her, but that would mean locking Solomon in her car, and he was still holding tight to her shoulder.

Moments later, a truck whipped into the drive. It stopped just short of Dorothy's little car. Hulda stepped out and ran around the side of the house.

"What are you doing here?" she seethed at Dorothy.

Dorothy's grip instinctively tightened around Solomon. "I could ask the same of you," Dorothy said. "I brought Solomon for a visit."

"Hulda," Sara said as she ran down the back steps, her baby still on her hip.

"*Segðu mér hvað gerðist,*" Hulda said as she pulled out a notebook.

"*Við vorum að pakka og – ég heyrði öskra. Isabelle er farin. Hún er farin, Hulda! Það var Yule kötturinn!*" She pointed a shaking finger at Solomon, and Dorothy took a step back.

"Would you wait out front?" Hulda asked Dorothy. "And do not go anywhere."

Dorothy raised an eyebrow at the woman. Hulda almost young enough to be her daughter. She hesitated, wondering if Hulda still carried the artifact in her pocket. She wasn't inclined to leave the woman alone with the family if she did, but Solomon was terrified.

Reluctantly, Dorothy nodded and headed for the warmth of her car. She opened the door, and Solomon immediately jumped inside. He paced from the dashboard to the rearview window, yowling and growling. Eventually, he settled into Dorothy's lap, though his ears continued to pivot as he listened intently.

A gentle snow was beginning to dust the little yellow car when Hulda closed the front door to the farmhouse behind her. She approached Dorothy's vehicle and motioned for her to step out.

Dorothy set Solomon on the passenger seat and stepped into the cold.

"You're with Caprice." It wasn't a question. Dorothy did not respond, but Hulda nodded. "Come with me. I think we can help each other."

SEVEN

SOLOMON LAY CURLED IN THE PASSENGER SEAT
of the car. Dorothy followed close behind Hulda's
truck, praying her car didn't fall apart as it bumped
and jerked over the uneven terrain.

After several miles, Hulda turned toward another
farmhouse that sat close to the main road. Solomon
barely lifted his head when Dorothy parked and
turned the car off.

"It's all right, little one," Dorothy said, petting the
cat gently between his ears. Solomon looked at her
and mewed quietly. She carefully picked him up and
tucked him into her jacket.

Hulda stood waiting on the front steps. She held the
front door open and ushered Dorothy and Solomon
inside.

Despite the afternoon sun outside, the house was

dark. Hulda hurried toward a table on the other side of the room. She pulled a lighter from her pocket and lit a glass oil lamp.

Dorothy watched as the contents of the home came into view with each lamp Hulda lit. An air mattress sat in one corner, piled with more layers of blankets and coats than Dorothy could count. The rest of the furniture had been covered in plastic.

Hulda picked up one of the lamps and headed for the kitchen.

"This way," she said curtly. Dorothy reached into her purse and pulled out a small keychain flashlight. She followed Hulda and stopped in the kitchen doorway.

It looked like a scene straight out of a television show, only more haphazard. Centrifuges, microscopes and machines of all kinds had been set up along the counter. The top of the kitchen table couldn't be found beneath the massive piles of papers, folders and books.

Hulda lit another lamp in the corner of the kitchen and pocketed the lighter.

"You will have to forgive the mess. The house has been abandoned for some time. There is no electricity here, so I apologize that it's so dark."

"What is all this?" Dorothy asked, shining her light over the makeshift laboratory.

Hulda sighed. "It would take too much time to send

samples all the way back to Reykjavík, so I set up a lab here. I use generators for my equipment. I majored in microbiology before earning my badge."

Hulda reached into the top pocket of her coat, and Dorothy felt herself instinctively hold tighter to Solomon. Hulda took several steps toward Dorothy and held out her hand. Slowly, Dorothy extended hers and Hulda dropped a heavy metal object into her palm.

Dorothy stared at it. Though the wording was in Icelandic, there was no questioning what it was.

"*You're* Detective Svanursdottir?"

Hulda reached into a cooler beneath the counter and grabbed two water bottles. She handed one to Dorothy, taking the badge back, then leaned against the counter and took a long drink.

"The very same," she said. "I am going to cut to the chase with you, as you say in America. I do not know what happened to Caprice, but if you do not wish to suffer the same fate, I suggest you take your little *köttur* and go back to the States. This does not concern you."

Solomon shifted inside Dorothy's coat. She loosened her grip but placed a protective hand across his shoulders. "Unfortunately, it involves me more than you think. Especially now that Caprice is missing as well."

Hulda raised an eyebrow at her. "Oh?"

"There are things in this world that are more dangerous than you could possibly imagine," Dorothy said.

The two women stared at each other. Apart from Solomon's shifting, the room was silent. After several moments, Hulda's lip curled into a smile.

"Right. Then we best get to work." She turned toward one of the machines and pulled a tiny bag from her pocket.

Dorothy stared at Hulda's back, unmoving. "That's it?" she asked.

Hulda continued to work, moving pieces of the machines with deliberate experience. "Caprice and I had been working together since she first arrived. She said the same thing to me, or close enough anyway. Something about powers falling into the wrong hands or some such. You want to save your friend, *já*?" She looked over her shoulder, a mischievous grin still playing on her face.

"Of course, I do," said Dorothy. "And save the other girls."

"Then hand me the sample of fur in your pocket. I do not have enough."

Dorothy furrowed her brow.

"How did –?"

"You left behind a thumbprint in the snow. I knew it was yours. I felt the shape of your hand and fingers when I came to your room last night."

This time, Dorothy smiled. She set the flashlight on the table and handed Hulda the chunk of fur she had retrieved from Solomon's mouth.

Solomon poked his head out of Dorothy's coat as the centrifuge began to spin down.

"Don't get into anything," Dorothy whispered to him. She unzipped her coat, and Solomon leapt to the floor.

Hulda turned when she felt him rub against her legs.

"It is a shame so many still let superstitions cloud their judgements," she said, kneeling to pet the cat. "He is a sweet boy."

"Most of the time," Dorothy said, sitting in one of the kitchen chairs. Driving with a manual transmission and clutch was beginning to make her knee cramp.

"He really climbed into your suitcase?" Hulda asked with a chuckle.

Dorothy rolled her eyes. "Unfortunately."

"And the airport did not catch him?"

Dorothy rubbed her knees, wishing she had applied some of her joint cream before leaving. "The organization Caprice and I work for doesn't always use the same public channels as everyone else."

Hulda's grin only deepened. She reached into her pocket, fidgeting with something as she had the night before. "I wish I had you and Caprice around before."

"Before what?" Dorothy asked.

Solomon batted at Hulda's hand, still clutched in her pocket.

"Never mind," she whispered. "We do not believe in trolls, remember?"

"Don't we?"

Hulda walked across the room and joined Dorothy at the table. She pulled her hand from her pocket and handed a tiny metal locket to Dorothy.

Dorothy took it gently as Solomon jumped into Hulda's lap. Inside was a picture of a dark-haired child snuggling with a puppy.

"Her name is Ann," Hulda said, her voice now low and quiet as she stroked Solomon in her lap.

"She's beautiful," Dorothy said, handing the locket back to Hulda.

The woman took it and traced her thumb across the front of the glass. "She is."

"Where is she?"

Hulda sighed and stared out one of the windows. "When the first two girls went missing, we thought we were seeing a pattern. The families were all in the process of downsizing from the farmhouses. Their most precious belongings were all in one place – the moving trucks – so they would have been easy targets for thieves. But it was not that simple."

"It never is," Dorothy said.

Hulda nodded and continued. "The trouble was, none of the valuables had been touched. Only the daughters. Everyone wants to blame the Yule cat, but…"

"But what do you think it is?"

"I think these poor girls have been targeted and rounded up for a very specific, very unspeakable purpose." Hulda clenched her jaw, her sadness turning to anger. "Humans are the vilest of creatures on this Earth. Not trolls or bloodthirsty cats. Only humans would think to profit off children."

The centrifuge on the counter slowed and came to a stop. It beeped loudly, and Solomon hurried across the room to investigate the sound.

Hulda stood and removed the vial inside. Carefully, she extracted some of the liquid the hair had been suspended in and placed it on a microscope slide.

Dorothy stood and watched as Hulda pulled away from the microscope, the color draining from her face. "I have only ever seen these results once before," she whispered.

"When? What is it?" Dorothy asked, stepping closer. She approached the microscope, reaching a hand to look through the lens, but she wouldn't have known what she was looking for.

Hulda began to pace, rubbing the back of the picture frame absentmindedly. She reached for her cell phone sitting on the counter and stared at the screen. "They will never believe me."

"Hulda, what's going on? Tell me," Dorothy urged, and Solomon meowed, as if agreeing.

Hulda looked at Dorothy. She opened her mouth to speak when the phone in her hand began to ring. She answered with trembling fingers.

"Halló?"

There was chatter on the other end that Dorothy couldn't make out. She sat in the kitchen chair again, her heart beating faster with each passing moment.

"Nei, gertu ekki þetta. Ég er nálægt!" Hulda clutched at Ann's picture, tears beginning to stream down her face. "Ekki gera þetta."

The phone clicked, and Hulda slowly lowered it.

"Hulda, what happened?" Dorothy asked.

Hulda turned, her bottom lip trembling. "They took me off the case," she whispered.

"Why? We can't give up. Those little girls are still out there! Isabelle just went missing not two hours ago!"

Hulda looked at the picture in her hand. A lone tear landed on the glass, and she quickly wiped it away.

"I think you should go," Hulda said, sinking into the kitchen chair.

"Hulda –"

"Just go! *Nuna!*"

Dorothy stood and gathered Solomon into her arms. "You know where to find me," she said. "I'm not giving up."

She zipped the little cat into her coat again and headed for her car.

EIGHT

DOROTHY SHOOK THE ENTIRE WAY BACK TO THE Kaffihúsið, and it wasn't just the cold. The farmhouse had been dark, giving the illusion that night had come. But the sun had barely begun to dip in the sky when Dorothy left. It was still plenty bright, even through the cloud cover. She was glad for it. She had no idea if she was still chasing an Icelandic legend like the townsfolk thought, or if her quarry was far more human.

The gravel crunched beneath the little car as Dorothy parked. Solomon stepped carefully onto her lap and waited for her to clip on his leash. She opened the door and grabbed him mid-leap as a van whipped into the parking lot beside her.

"*Fyrirgefðu!*" A woman stepped from the vehicle and ran to Dorothy. "I am sorry," she repeated in English.

Dorothy caught her breath, and Solomon wiggled in

her arms. "It's all right. I caught him."

"You are the American who is staying here," the woman said.

Dorothy nodded.

"Not exactly what you expected." The woman gestured toward the bed and breakfast.

Dorothy glanced over her shoulder and watched as a burly man dragged a mattress through the front doors.

"I never know what to expect when I travel," she replied, finally giving in to Solomon's wiggles and protests. He immediately ran to the woman and head-bonked her shins. "If there's anything I can do to help, let me know."

"If you can spare the time, we need more people on watch shifts."

"Watch shifts?" Dorothy asked.

The woman nodded as Solomon sniffed at her pant leg, opening his mouth to smell more deeply.

"We are stationing people inside and out all night. Nothing is going to take our children." She reached into the front seat of her car, pulling out a large bag. "Some of us have already placed offerings to Gryla and the Yule cat by the mountain."

Solomon sneezed and trotted back to Dorothy.

"I'm sure I can spare a few hours," Dorothy said.

The woman smiled weakly. "*Þakka þér fyrir.* You will want to speak with Natan. He is organizing everything."

"Of course." Dorothy smiled reassuringly, then tugged on Solomon's leash, heading for the front door.

There was more activity in the restaurant than Dorothy would have guessed. Filip had made quick work of clearing out the space, and it was now full of mattresses, cots and sleeping bags. Children were running back and forth between the rows of beds, and the adults were pointing and yelling, seemingly trying to figure out how to cram more beds into the tiny space.

Solomon stared longingly at the throng of people. He meowed at Dorothy, turning in a circle and pulling against the leash.

"Dorothy," said a voice through the crowd. Filip shouldered his way over, waving through an armful of blankets. "The kitchen will open in an hour. Can I bring you anything?"

"You look busy enough without having to wait on me," Dorothy said. "Is there a store close by I can find something at?"

Filip waved his hand before him, silencing her. "My guests will not be subjected to protein bars and chips. I will bring you something nice." With that, he turned back toward the chaos in the restaurant, adjusting the blankets in his arms.

After much prompting from Dorothy, Solomon bounded up the narrow staircase, threatening to pull the leash out of her hands. When they reached the room, he dove under the bed, trilling and mewing excitedly.

Dorothy dropped the leash and immediately kicked off her shoes. She pushed Caprice's bag aside and stretched out on the bed, her conversation with Hulda running rampant through her mind.

Two days. She had only been here for two days, but it felt like so much longer. She was exhausted and felt no closer to finding Caprice or the missing children than when she'd first arrived.

She felt Solomon jump onto the bed and heard his gentle purrs as he snuggled up beside her. She wrapped her arm around him, her eyelids growing heavier by the moment. Solomon's purrs seemed to change. More rhythmic, more… like a buzzing sound.

Dorothy's eyes shot open. She swung her legs over the side of the bed and pulled out her suitcase. She opened it, digging through the piles of thermal underwear until she found her tablet. She quickly swiped at the green button, and Destin's face appeared on the screen before her again.

"Please tell me you found something," Dorothy said before he could speak.

"Hello to you too, Fennec. Why don't you tell me what you found first?" Destin asked, raising his eyebrow at her.

"Not much. There's something I'm missing, but I have no idea what it is. Another little girl was taken this afternoon, in broad daylight, Destin. Solomon went after something –"

"Solomon? Your cat is with you?"

Dorothy's cheeks flushed. "Yes. He climbed inside my suitcase," she said for what felt like the thousandth time.

Destin lowered his head to his hands. "Fennec, I cannot have you compromised from finding Caprice because of you being concerned about the safety of your cat."

"He's fine, Destin. If anything, he's helped. But I need to know if you found anything about that warehouse. Another child goes missing every day."

"Have you found anything that could lead to Caprice?"

Dorothy sat straighter. "Are you listening to me? Children are disappearing."

"I just need you to find Caprice," Destin pressed.

"Destin, what is going on? You're not the least bit

concerned about these kids."

"No, it's not like that." Destin held up his hands in defense. "Fennec, I'm dealing with a lot right now, and it's vital we find Caprice."

"I understand. I'm worried about her too. But I think if I can finish solving this case, it will lead to her. So please tell me you found something out about that warehouse."

Destin sifted through a stack of paper, and Dorothy watched as it cascaded to the floor. Destin cried out angrily and disappeared under his desk. After several moments, she saw his head pop up, his hair as disheveled as when she'd seen him yesterday.

"Let me get back to you on that, Fennec." He reached forward, pushing a button and ending the call.

Dorothy jumped when she felt something touch her back. Solomon pawed at her, then proceeded to jump on her shoulder. He meowed, staring at the blank tablet on the woman's lap. She flicked on the side lamp and placed the tablet back into her suitcase once more.

Solomon leapt from her shoulder, landing on the suitcase, and allowing himself to be pushed under the bed with it. Dorothy shook her head and glanced at her watch.

Iceland was four hours ahead of the East Coast.

Aaron would still be at work. She pulled out her phone and dialed the number for the antique shop.

"Thank you for calling Richard's Anecdotes. This is Aaron. How may I help you?" came Aaron's soft tone.

"Hello, Aaron. It's Dorothy."

"Ms. Claes! Is Solomon doing all right? I can't imagine him being trapped in your suitcase through an entire plane ride."

Dorothy smiled as Solomon dug his way out from under the bed, his whiskers covered in cobwebs. "He's perfectly fine. How are things with the shop?"

"A bit slow. We're still digging out from that storm." Aaron let out a shuttering breath.

"Did Mr. Jacobs call to arrange dropping off his Da Vinci drawings?"

"No, ma'am. Do you really think they're genuine?"

Dorothy stifled a laugh. "No, but it doesn't mean we won't take a look at them and appraise them for him. He's paying regardless."

"I understand. Oh, someone did come in this morning, ma'am," Aaron said excitedly. "A man wanted to talk to you about some health records."

The hair on Dorothy's neck stood on end. Her grip tightened on the phone. "What did he say?" she asked.

"Nothing really, ma'am. Since you're gone, I asked him where you could reach him. He gave me a card, but it only has a phone number on it. It seems a bit strange, ma'am."

"It is strange. I'll take care of it when I'm back. Give Mr. Jacobs a call again if you would. Let me know if anything else comes up."

"Will do, ma'am. Give Solomon a good chin scratch from me. I've been worried about him."

As if on cue, Solomon leapt onto the bed. Dorothy scratched his chin as instructed and replied, "I will. Good-bye, Aaron."

Solomon leaned into Dorothy's hand, then whipped around to face the door. He covered the length of the room in two long strides and stuck his nose under the door. A soft knock greeted him, and Dorothy stood to answer.

Filip stood outside the door, a tray of food in hand.

"I thought you said the kitchen didn't open for an hour," Dorothy said, taking the tray from the man while attempting to keep Solomon inside the room with her foot. She was unsuccessful, but Filip gently gathered the cat into his arms and followed Dorothy into the room.

"I wanted to ask if you had found anything. If you had found your friend." Filip's voice was low as he set Solomon on the bed.

Dorothy placed the tray on the dresser and turned

back to Filip. "I have some leads I'm working on, but no, nothing yet."

Filip hung his head and nodded. "It's just as well," he said.

"But I still want to help." Dorothy set a hand on Filip's shoulder. "I want to take one of the watch shifts tonight."

Filip's face brightened. "I will let Natan know. He is working on a schedule. Thank you, Dorothy." He clasped Dorothy's hands between his and squeezed. "Ah, was Ada's book helpful?"

Dorothy blinked, confused by the sudden change in subject. Filip gestured to the book on the nightstand that Solomon was now perched upon.

"Oh, yes. Yes, it was," Dorothy replied. She reached over, dislodging the little cat and handing it to Filip. "She said to give it to you when I was finished."

Filip took the book, and a small card fell out of its pages. Solomon pounced at it, pinning the card to the floor. The man wrestled the card from the cat's paws and handed it to Dorothy.

"She put her latest video up today if you would like to watch it." Filip handed the card to Dorothy. It was the card Ada had given her with her web address.

"That sounds perfect," Dorothy said.

NINE

WITH THE KAFFIHÚSIÐ OVERRUN WITH GUESTS, most of the hot water had been depleted. Dorothy wiped down with a washcloth, changed into clean clothes, and climbed beneath the covers. She had a few hours before her shift. Natan wanted the parents to sleep with their children and had asked anyone else available to take watch through the night.

Dorothy pulled the tray of food onto her lap and used her Foxes tablet to navigate to Ada's website. *Bókfíkillinn*, the banner at the top read. "The Book Addict." She clicked on the *play* button for the video and dug in to her food.

At first, Dorothy thought she may have gone to the wrong website, but there was no mistaking the armchair or the enormous bookshelf behind it. Ada sat perched on the chair, an excited smile spread across her face.

"Welcome back, book addicts! Today we're going to be discussing the legend of *Jólasveinarnir*." She held up a book and flipped her long hair behind her.

Dorothy grinned. This was a completely different Ada. She looked at the count below the video. Two million subscribers. The video had only been uploaded six hours ago, and already it had over three thousand views.

Ada bounced in the chair. "If you're not from Iceland, and most of you are not, then you probably don't know about *Jólasveinarnir*, or the Yule lads. So, let me give you a little backstory before we dive into this book."

The video and music changed, launching into what appeared to be an animated video, complete with an upbeat tune.

"Every year, Iceland is subjected to the antics of the twelve lads of Christmas. Each day, starting on December twelfth, a different lad crosses into the world of mortals and plays tricks on them. You have *Stekkjarstaur*, the sheep-cote clod. He harasses the sheep, but he has these little peg legs, so he can't get around very well. *Giljagaur*, or the Gully-Gawk, waits in gullies for the opportunity to jump out and steal milk from the milking sheds. There's *Hurðaskellir* the

Door-Slammer and *Gluggagægir* the Window-Peeper. I'm not going to go into every single one, but if you're interested, I have some links listed below. And don't worry, they're in English, so all my non-Icelandic speaking followers, I got you covered."

Dorothy watched and listened as Ada flashed her smile and flipped her hair. She talked about the book she had up at the beginning of the video in great detail. Dorothy was impressed. Solomon finished his dinner and joined Dorothy on the bed as she finished her own meal.

"If you're interested in purchasing a copy of the book, you can find a link for that listed below as well. And if you have any information on the missing children of Eskifjorður, please call the phone number here. That's all I have for you this week! I'm just finishing up a novel from Auður Ava Ólafsdóttir, and I should have it done in time for our next video. Until next time. *Hamingjusamur lestur!*"

The video ended, and Ada's logo swirled across the screen. Solomon batted at it and launched one of the links in the process. Dorothy quickly snatched the tablet away.

"I'm sorry, little one, but it's time to –"

Solomon's pupil's dilated. He flattened himself on the bed, a low growl shaking his entire body. Dorothy followed his gaze to the door. There was a soft knock, and Solomon disappeared under the bed.

As quietly as her creaking joints would let her, Dorothy slipped from beneath the covers and pulled the gun out of her purse.

"Who is it?" she asked when she reached the door.

"Hulda," came the strained whisper.

"Hulda?" Dorothy opened the door, her gun still clutched tightly in her hand. "What are you doing here?"

"I had nowhere else to go. Please, can I come in?"

Dorothy held the door open and quickly shut it behind the woman. "What's going on?"

Hulda looked dazed. Her dark hair was a tangled mess, and blood seeped from her arm beneath the hand that clutched it.

Dorothy sprang into action. She soaked a hand towel in the bathroom sink and handed it to the woman.

"What happened?" Dorothy demanded.

Hulda gingerly removed her hand, wincing at the pain. Dorothy gasped when she saw the long, deep gashes in her arm. Hulda dabbed at the wounds with the cloth, her hands shaking.

"Hulda?" Dorothy prompted.

Hulda tossed the cloth on the floor, and Solomon poked his head out from under the bed to sniff it. The little cat glanced up at Hulda and disappeared under the bed again.

"I don't know if you would believe me if I told you," Hulda whispered, not daring to meet Dorothy's eye.

Solomon growled from beneath the bed. It was the same way he had growled at Hulda their first night, and the way he had growled after Isabelle had been taken.

"Let's get you cleaned up," Dorothy said. She led Hulda to the bathroom and laid out one of her nightdresses for her to wear. She gathered Hulda's clothes, carefully looking at the sleeves of her jacket. Whatever had attacked Hulda had barely been halted by her heavy winter coat.

Dorothy quickly snapped some pictures of the damage and shoved Hulda's dirty clothes into the closet.

It took quite a bit of coaxing and an entire tin of canned food for Dorothy to get Solomon to come out from under the bed. By the time Hulda had showered and stepped into the room, a towel wrapped around her hair, the little cat was sleeping on the pillows once more.

Dorothy swung her legs over the side of the bed and gestured for Hulda to sit.

Hulda reached a hand toward her arm again.

She stood framed in the bathroom doorway, as if contemplating her next move. Eventually, she sat beside Dorothy. She still would not look at the old woman. She shuffled her feet like a child and studied the floor.

Dorothy wished she had tea, but she didn't want to disturb the families who were beginning to settle in for the night. Instead, she gently rubbed Hulda's back, patiently waiting for her to speak.

"What do you think of fairy tales and superstitions, Dorothy?" Hulda finally asked.

Dorothy did not pause in her gentle strokes across Hulda's back as she replied, "I believe there must be some level of truth to them. How else would they have come into existence?"

Hulda nodded and shuffled her feet again. The towel was beginning to loosen around her head, and a single lock of dark hair fell out.

"I was packing up my equipment. Most of the oil lamps had burned up shortly after you left, so I was in a hurry to finish before the rest went out. It was so strange. There was no sound, but I knew."

"Knew what?" Dorothy asked.

"That something was watching me." She rose from the bed and began pacing the room, her voice becoming tighter by the moment. "I looked out the window and… and something was standing in the field. It was huge. Just a mass of black, but it was blacker than the night. I couldn't see its eyes, but I felt it. It was watching me. I grabbed my gun and tried to call my boss. But the line was completely dead. Then I heard something at the door. A… like a scratching. But the black figure was still there. I was trapped. I knew if I took my eyes off that…*thing*…to lock the door that it would move. But I had to barricade the door. The scratching stopped for several minutes, and I watched the light of the last oil lamp grow dimmer. As soon as it went out, something rushed the door. It… It attacked me."

Hulda raised a hand to the back of her neck. Carefully, Dorothy pulled the dressing gown back and saw several large punctures.

"Something tried to drag you off," Dorothy said.

"I was able to get off two shots. I have no idea if I hit anything, but it and the dark figure were gone."

A muffled buzzing made both women jump. Solomon sat up with a trill and immediately leapt from the bed. He pawed at Dorothy's suitcase until the woman opened it and retrieved the tablet inside.

The text across the front read *Destin*, and Dorothy immediately swiped to answer the call.

The face that greeted her was not Destin.

"Jorge?" Dorothy asked.

The short, Brazilian man jumped and quickly dismissed the call. Dorothy's screen turned black again.

"Who was that?" Hulda asked.

"Jorge. One of our – my colleagues. What was he doing at headquarters?"

"Headquarters?"

The tablet buzzed again, and Destin's name appeared once more. Dorothy swiped and was greeted by Destin's familiar face.

"Fennec," he greeted her.

"Destin, what was Jorge doing there just now?"

Destin's brow furrowed and his face blanched. "Jorge? Was here?"

Dorothy matched Destin's confused expression. "You didn't know?"

Destin waved a dismissive hand, but his voice remained tense. "I have the information you asked for." He pulled a piece of paper across the desk and leaned in to read. "The warehouse is registered under the company name of g-g... *Gluggagægir*. It's a shipping company for windows. The owner is listed as Galdur Glugga, but I couldn't find any contact information."

"*Gluggagægir*," Dorothy repeated. "Why is that

familiar?" She looked over her shoulder at Hulda. Solomon had positioned himself on the woman's lap, accepting her pets and purring with delight. Hulda looked anything but delighted.

"I don't know, Fennec. That's what you're there to figure out. Is there anything else I can do for you?"

"No. Thank you, Destin."

"Find her, Fennec. Find her and get out of there."

Once more, Dorothy was left staring at a black screen. Solomon stood from Hulda's lap and mewed pitifully at Dorothy. He batted at the screen until Dorothy turned on his favorite mouse-catching app. She set it on the pillow behind her and turned to Hulda.

"You know that name," she said. "Why?"

Hulda took a deep breath. "When I was a little girl, I used to sneak into the kitchen after my family was asleep. My mother made the most delicious sweets for Christmas. I never knew why, but... I knew there was something. Something watching me. I couldn't tell my parents. I would have to tell them about stealing the sweets. Not that they didn't already know." Hulda shifted uncomfortably on the bed. "Once, I looked through the kitchen window and I saw someone, some*thing* staring back at me. That was when I told my father. He said it was *Gluggagægir*, the Window-Peeper. One of the twelve trolls of Christmas."

"You saw this Window-Peeper?" Dorothy asked. Solomon pounced on the tablet screen, completely flipping it over. He yowled in frustration, and Dorothy quickly righted it. "What did he look like?"

Hulda shook her head. "I-I do not remember. Not like that. It is not how you think. It followed me for years. Even after I was too old to believe in the superstitions. After I had moved out of my parents' home. My apartment at Uni was on the third floor, but I would still find these massive footprints on my windowsill.

"I was scared. My ex-husband said I was paranoid. Every window in my home was blocked with heavy curtains. I installed additional locks on every door and window. When Ann started to see it as well, he tried to use my paranoia against me to take her from me. It didn't work, thank God. But three years ago, she disappeared."

Hulda reached for the locket with the picture of Ann in her pocket. "The police were convinced she had been targeted for trafficking. They would not let me near the case. When the situation here came across my desk, I begged my supervisor to let me take it."

She looked up, her eyes brimming with tears. "It will not stop until it has me. I will do anything, *anything*, to get my daughter back, Dorothy." Hulda took a ragged breath and reached for her injured arm again. She shook her head and sniffed. "You probably think I am crazy."

Dorothy cleared her throat, though her voice threatened to crack. She wiped her eyes before Hulda could see her and replied, "I absolutely believe you, Hulda."

Hulda turned quickly back to Dorothy, her red eyes wide with disbelief. "You do?"

Dorothy nodded. "I do. Whatever this thing is, it's why I'm here. It's why Caprice was here. We'll find it, Hulda."

Someone knocked quietly on the door, making both women jump. They hadn't noticed Solomon had already assumed his position, sniffing at the gap beneath the door. Dorothy rose and opened it.

"Dorothy?" It was Natan.

"Yes. Is everything all right?"

Natan nodded and continued in a whisper. "Your shift is starting. We have some families staying in some of the rooms. Would you be willing to monitor the hall?"

"Of course. I'll be right there."

Natan nodded, and Dorothy closed the door behind him, Solomon wiggling in her arms.

"You're taking a watch shift?" Hulda asked.

"Of course, I am," Dorothy said. She set Solomon on the bed and reached for her purse. She pulled out her Smith & Wesson and checked that the chamber was fully loaded.

"Let me come with you. Let me help," Hulda pleaded.

Dorothy set a hand on the woman's shoulder, urging her to remain seated. "You need to rest."

"But –"

Dorothy held up her hand. "No buts. Rest." She gestured toward the bed, where Solomon had resumed his post on the pillow. Hulda looked tentatively at her injured arm. "Solomon can sense whatever this thing is. He'll protect you."

"Your *cat* will protect me?" Hulda asked, raising an eyebrow.

Dorothy smirked. "If Solomon can survive being imprisoned in the Egyptian underworld, he can warn you when this Yule cat is close by."

Hulda's mouth dropped open a bit. Dorothy removed her hand from the woman's shoulder and headed into the darkness of the hall.

TEN

THERE WERE THREE MORE GUEST ROOMS AT THE Kaffihúsið in addition to Dorothy's room. All of them had been packed full of families and children, the doors and windows locked tight.

Despite the darkness and the still of the night, the inn was restless. Little ones could be heard crying, and everyone tossed and turned on their mattresses and cots. Dorothy sat in one of the restaurant chairs that had been brought up to the hallway. The wood creaked beneath her almost as much as her knees and elbows. She could feel the temperature outside dropping quickly and had seen snow begin to fall again through the window when she had peeked in at Hulda.

The woman slept with her arm curled around Solomon, and the little cat seemed to have snuggled into her protectively. He lifted his head and blinked once at Dorothy as she quietly closed the door once more.

That had been an hour ago. Dorothy flexed her fingers and moved her joints. She tried to stay as quiet as possible, but her bones and the cold had other ideas. The anticipation of another child being taken lingered throughout the place. She could hear muffled whispers and pacing from the first floor below.

Isabelle had been taken in broad daylight, but she had been the tenth child. With the pattern being only one child missing per day, would the Yule cat dare to steal another before dawn?

She took a deep breath and stood. She couldn't sit any longer. She needed to get her blood flowing. Even through three layers of socks, her toes were freezing. She walked the length of the hall, pausing and listening at each door. A little girl whispered in the darkness, something Dorothy couldn't understand. A woman's voice replied, consoling the child.

Dorothy swallowed and moved on. She stopped at the base of the stairs, peering down at the check-in stand.

"Filip?" Dorothy called into the darkness.

Hurried footsteps echoed in the dark, and a silhouette appeared at the base of the stairs.

"Dorothy?" Filip asked, and Dorothy could feel the

tension in his voice.

"I just wondered if I could get some more water," she whispered back.

The silhouette's head moved in a nodding motion, then turned away from the stairs.

A creature screamed into the night, and the cries of the once-sleeping children answered. Dorothy had heard that sound once before. She tore back up the hall, ignoring the heads that poked out from the other rooms. She raced to the end of the hall and wretched open the door to her own room.

Solomon stood on the bed, hissing and spitting at the now-open window. Hulda was gone. Footsteps pounded up the stairs as Filip and two other men joined her. Dorothy gripped her gun and edged toward the open window. The freshly fallen snow was completely undisturbed, save for a single, large pawprint on the sill. It was easily the size of a bear's – exactly like the one she had found earlier.

"*Hvað gerðist?*" one of the men said, his eyes turning sharply to Dorothy. He moved toward her, covering the distance of the small room in a single stride. He grabbed her shoulders, and Dorothy could feel his grip tighten. She pressed the barrel of her gun into his chest, and he quickly drew away.

"Dorothy," Filip said from the door. "What

happened?"

Dorothy lowered her gun. She looked at the window, then at Solomon, who had flattened himself on the bed and had resorted to a low growl again.

"There was no warning," she said.

"You left your watch," the second man behind Filip snapped. "You are working with –"

Filip held up his hand. *"Láttu hana tala."*

"I paused at every door. There was nothing until -" Dorothy swallowed, recalling the ear-piercing scream of whatever had taken Hulda. "We have to go after her."

"Are all Americans as crazy as you?" the first man asked. "We stay here. Remember, Isabelle was taken in broad daylight today. Our children are not safe until that *thing* is killed!" He threw his hands in the air and stormed out of the room, pushing his way past the crowd of people who had gathered in the hall.

Dorothy turned and slammed the window shut, watching as tufts of snow sprayed across the floor. Hulda's locket lay beneath the window, the glass inside cracked across Ann's picture. She lifted it gently, and snapped the locket shut.

"That thing has been after Hulda since she was a child," Dorothy said, her voiced raised so everyone in the hall could hear her. "Her own daughter was taken by whatever this is years ago."

"She should have turned herself over to it sooner, then!" one of the women in the hall said. "If it is her it's been after, then let it have her!"

Several onlookers nodded and shouted their agreements.

"And how do you know it *will* stop at Hulda?" came a younger voice. The crowd turned and stared at Ada. The girl's hair was tangled, and her mascara had smeared beneath her eyes, but she stood as determined as the rest. "Hulda risked her life to come here, to save our children. We can't abandon her now."

She flashed a smile at Dorothy, who stood dumbfounded, staring back.

"No," someone in the back said. "I will not leave my baby." With that, the crowd slowly dispersed.

"Filip," Dorothy pleaded as the man turned to leave. "We can't leave her."

Filip sighed scratching at his back. "It's not for me to say," he said, and left, closing the door behind him.

Dorothy dropped to the bed, her gun still held tight in her hands. She tossed it in her purse. A lot of good it had done. Hot tears stung her eyes. Hulda had been the closest she had come to answers since accepting her mission. For a brief moment, Dorothy thought she had finally found the key to saving Caprice, to saving the lost girls.

Solomon's growl intensified. The hair along his back stood straight. He stalked across the bed, staring at the blackness of the window.

Red's words echoed in Dorothy's mind. "Do you smell something, little one?"

Solomon sat beneath the window, his tail flicking madly. He leapt onto the windowsill and began pawing feverishly at the glass. Dorothy stepped toward the window. Through the darkness the silhouette of the Hólmatindur mountain loomed in the distance.

Despite her lack of sleep and the cold that seemed to grip her like a vise, Dorothy's mind began to race. She covered the length of the room and pulled open the door. A few parents remained in the hall outside. They ceased their conversation, their glares landing heavily on Dorothy.

"What are you doing?" one of them asked, her voice as icy as the snow that still fell outside.

Dorothy pushed past them.

"*Hvert ertu að fara?*" another shouted, but Dorothy ignored them.

She tore down the narrow staircase as quickly as her knees would allow. Filip stood beside the check-in stand, Natan and the two men who had stormed Dorothy's room at his side.

"Filip," Dorothy said, reaching for the man's hand. "Where's Ada?"

"Ada?"

"Yes. Is she still here?"

"Uh – she – "

"I'm here," said Ada's voice from the restaurant.

Dorothy pushed her way through the men. Even in the semi-darkness, she could see Ada's frown had returned.

"Ada, I need your help."

"Me?" Ada pulled away. "What do you want with me? I'm not sacrificing myself if that's –"

"No!" one of the men shouted.

Dorothy held up a hand, halting the man. "Ada," she said, "you're the smartest person here when it comes to Icelandic lore."

"What? No, I –"

"She's right," Filip said. "You have read every one of those books. You know everything that's in them."

"What does that matter?" the man Dorothy still held at arm's length spat.

"Because if it's the Yule Lads and the Yule cat who have taken your girls, we need someone who understands them."

"*Þetta er fáranlegt*," a woman in the restaurant entrance said.

"Do you have a better suggestion?" Filip asked.

Silence. Only the sound of the creaking floorboards beneath their feet gave any indication of life in the dark room.

"Okay, fine," Ada said, throwing her hands in the air. "But how do we even know where to find them?"

Dorothy felt a grin spread across her face. "I know someone who can."

"Your *cat*." Ada stood in the guest room doorway, slack-jawed as Dorothy adjusted Solomon's harness.

"Yes," Dorothy repeated for the second time.

"You want me to follow your *cat* into a mountain to find trolls."

Dorothy sighed. "He's – He's not a typical cat."

"I can see this." Ada crossed her arms before her. "But he's a *cat*."

Dorothy zipped her coat and reached for Solomon's leash. "Ada, have you ever been to a Tibetan monastery? Eaten with the monks and sat with them during their morning prayers?" Ada shifted uncomfortably beneath Dorothy's gaze. "Have you ever walked the Great Wall of China or been caught in the middle of a pod of dolphins in nothing more than a kayak?"

"No, but –"

"Have you ever been trapped between the world of the living and the dead by an Egyptian guardian of the underworld?"

"What?" Ada's gaze fell to Solomon, who would not budge from his post at the window. His tail swished back and forth, as agitated as any normal cat.

"Solomon has lived through more than you could possibly imagine. He knows something that we don't. The three of us together are the best chance this town has of saving those girls." Dorothy scooped up the little cat. He gave a low growl and buried his face in the crook of her arm . "You're either coming or staying, but I'm leaving right now."

"Wait!" Ada held up her hands and Dorothy moved toward the door. "Are you serious? He did all that?"

Dorothy sighed. The globetrotting might have been easy to believe, but even Dorothy would have had a hard time knowing her cat had been trapped by an Egyptian guardian if she hadn't seen it with her own eyes.

"Does it matter?" she asked.

"Of course, it matters!"

Dorothy opened the door to the closet and pulled out Hulda's coat.

"Seeing is believing, right?" Dorothy pushed past Ada and headed down the narrow staircase.

ELEVEN

DOROTHY OPENED THE TRUNK TO HER RICKETY rental car and tossed Hulda's coat in the back. Solomon's face was still buried in arms. She hoped this would work.

She opened the driver's side door and climbed in. Solomon eased into the passenger seat. He looked around cautiously, his movements slow and deliberate.

The snow was continuing to fall, but it wasn't heavy. Dorothy turned the ignition and flipped on the wipers. In the distance, she saw Ada run out the front door of the Kaffihúsið waving her arms above her head and balancing a bag on her back.

"Wait!" she called as she threw open the passenger door. "I'm coming," she said, out of breath.

Dorothy nodded and put on her seatbelt. Ada climbed in the car and tried to put on her own belt as Solomon crawled on her lap.

"What's in the bag?" Dorothy asked as she carefully pulled out of the gravel parking lot. The snow was light and powdery, and deceptively slick. She drove as quickly as she dared, farther out of town, and closer to the mountain.

"Offerings," Ada replied. She reached over Solomon and into the bag. She pulled out a small bottle of milk, a container of skyr, and even a long, wooden spoon. "I couldn't able to find things for each of them. You know, there wasn't time to strap a door to the car."

Ada screamed as Dorothy turned off the road, heading toward the looming mountain. "What are you doing?" she cried.

"I don't know about you, but these old bones would prefer to do as little walking as possible."

Ada wrapped one arm around Solomon, holding him close to her chest. The other clutched at the handle assist as Dorothy maneuvered the car closer to the mountain.

The terrain began to slope, and the car jerked and bounced vivaciously, causing Ada to squeak with each bump. Dorothy felt the car begin to give way. It chugged and stopped, the tires still spinning in the snow.

"Crap," Dorothy murmured.

Ada loosened her grip on Solomon, and the cat

darted toward the window, pawing and pressing his nose against the glass.

"Is this it?" Ada asked.

Dorothy grabbed the end of Solomon's leash and gathered the cat into her arms.

"This is where we begin walking," she said, stepping out into the snow.

It was much deeper than the drifts back in town. The snow came almost to Dorothy's knee. The snow melted down her boots as she reached for Hulda's coat and held it up for Solomon to sniff. The little cat tried to push the coat away. He struggled against her grip and growled.

"Now where do we go?" Ada asked as she adjusted the pack on her back.

"Up," Dorothy said. She pulled the little keychain flashlight from her pocket and lifted her wet foot out of the snow.

The closer they came to the mountain, the less the snow had fallen. Soon, Dorothy gave in to Solomon's protests and followed close behind as he bounded through the snow.

"There are some caves farther up," Ada said when they had almost reached the mountain. "We used to play in them as kids, but we'd have to climb to get there."

Solomon stopped, and the two humans followed suit. His ears twitched wildly, and the hair along his spine slowly rose as he looked around.

Without warning, he bolted, pulling the leash from Dorothy's hand.

"Solomon!" she screamed before hurrying after him.

Dorothy and Ada watched as he seemingly ran headlong into the mountain face and disappeared.

Ada stopped, but Dorothy continued her pace. She held her hand in front of her and passed straight through the rock before her.

She gasped and stumbled when she found herself in a large tunnel. The flashlight passed over the stone walls. Nordic runes had been painted in a circle around the entrance Dorothy had just entered through. Ada stood outside, searching for the door Dorothy and Solomon had just disappeared through.

Dorothy turned, shining the light again farther into the cave. Solomon was nowhere to be found.

"Solomon," she called, and heard her voice echo deep into the mountain.

She turned back toward the entrance and stepped through. Ada shrieked and fell back into the snow.

"I would highly recommend *not* doing that once you get inside," Dorothy said. She grabbed Ada's hand, pulling her to her feet and through the entrance.

Ada was at least successful in not screaming. But the moment Dorothy pulled her through, she tripped on the dry, stone floor and fell flat on her face. She pushed herself to her knees and turned to look at the opening behind her.

"What…?"

"My guess is a magical illusion," Dorothy said. "See the runes? Come on. Solomon couldn't have gone far."

They crept quietly along the winding tunnel, Ada now holding a hand to her mouth to stifle any squeaks. The flashlight fell across stalactites and stalagmites that made the shadows move and dance ominously.

Despite the seeming normalcy of the cave, there loomed the ever-present reminder that they had entered through some kind of magical doorway. There was no way to tell what hid in the darkness.

The tunnel turned sharply and ended in a large cavern that connected thirteen additional tunnels. Dorothy stopped, shining her light at the entrance to each. There was still no sign of Solomon.

"Solomon," she whispered again into the dark. She paused, waiting for the little cat's familiar chirps and trills. Silence. "Solomon?" she repeated more desperately. Nothing.

Ada had bent over at the entrance to one of the caves and picked something up from the floor.

"Hey, look at this," she called.

Dorothy turned the light toward Ada and accepted the brass door knob she held out to her.

"What's this?" Dorothy asked, her voice strained. She was sure she would have found Solomon by now.

"There are dozens of them," Ada said.

Dorothy shined the light farther down the tunnel. As Ada had said, the edges were lined with dozens of door knobs. Glass seemed the most popular, but there were plenty of brass and wooden knobs as well.

Ada pushed past Dorothy and peered down the next tunnel.

"Here," she called. "Shine your light down here."

"We don't have time for this," Dorothy snipped, but she turned her light down the second tunnel. Tufts of wool, full coats of shorn sheep skin, and even a ram's skull littered the walkway.

"I know what this is," Ada said. She reached into her bag and pulled out the book she had recently reviewed. "I think these are the entrances to each of the lad's caves." She led Dorothy to each cave entrance, finding spoons, strange little pots, and containers of spoiled skyr.

"Look!" Ada said as they inspected another tunnel. Pieces of windows and panes of stained glass had been meticulously arranged along the edges of the tunnel;

some even hung on the stone or had been placed on glass shelves.

"*Gluggagægir*," Ada and Dorothy said together.

"This must be the way," Ada said, taking a step down the tunnel.

"Wait!" Dorothy said. Her voice echoed down the tunnel, making both she and Ada stop until the sound had faded. "If it was the Yule cat who was stealing the girls, this may not be the right way. Your book said the cat was owned by Gryla?"

Ada stepped out of the tunnel and began looking over her shoulder with a nervous tick. "You do not want to encounter Gryla," she said, her voice low and warning.

"Well, I don't necessarily want to encounter one of these Yule Lads, either, but –"

Ada shook her head. Even in the dim light of the tiny flashlight, Dorothy could see the worry on her face. "The Yule Lads are tricksters, pranksters. They cause mischief and inconveniences. Gryla is a true monster. She is said to steal children and eat them alive. We'd be like two chickens that walked into a chef's kitchen and roosted on the stove."

Dorothy narrowed her eyes. "Hold on. If Gryla eats children, and she owns the Yule cat that you all believe has been taking the children, then why suspect the

Yule Lads?"

"Some of us did think it was Gryla, but there were too many. She is said to have a veracious appetite, but nothing like this. It had to be something else. Something connected to the season, and the only connection was the Yule Lads. You're American. I understand your confusion."

"I may be American, but I can understand well enough," Dorothy said.

She turned from Ada, shining her flashlight over each tunnel entrance. Where was Solomon when she needed him?

"Stop," Ada said, pushing the flashlight in Dorothy's hand away from the tunnel. An orange glow brightened into view from deep in one of the tunnels. Dorothy quickly flicked the flashlight off, and the two hurried back down the tunnel they had entered from.

"I don't want to wait for my day to pick my bride!" said a gruff voice. "It's not fair."

"It was my idea, so you'll do as I say!" said another voice.

"What if Mum finds out?"

"She won't find out. Not until they agree to the terms."

"Yes," said the first voice. "Once the contracts are signed, they will be immortal. Mum can't say *no* then."

Dorothy wasn't sure what she expected if she met the Yule Lads. She imagined the trolls she had seen in picture books as a child. Slightly humanoid creatures with drooling mouths filled with pointed teeth and bright yellow eyes. What she certainly had not expected was the level of intelligence she was hearing in the conversation, and she wasn't sure which version frightened her more.

"But what are we going to do about the other one?" a new voice asked.

"I told you!" cried the first one. There was a scuffle and a shriek before the first voice continued. "We'll give her to Mum to eat when we tell her about the brides."

"But she is too old! She's too tough. You know Mum likes her meat tender," said the second voice.

"Then we will have to tenderize it for her first."

The trolls' laughter echoed throughout the caves. Dorothy could feel Ada trembling beside her. She laid a gentle hand on her back. Moments later, she squeaked.

The laughter died instantly.

"What was that?" one of the voices asked.

"Sounded like someone at the front door," said another.

Dorothy felt a gentle pressure against her legs. She

bent down and felt cloth straps over soft fur. She quickly gathered Solomon into her arms and tucked him into her coat.

The orange light was growing brighter. Ada shrunk back along the tunnel. Dorothy turned in time to see her slip and fall with a loud thud.

"Oy!" cried one of the voices. The sound of large, bare feet slapping the stone floor echoed throughout the cave.

Ada scrambled to her feet and bolted for the portal entrance before Dorothy could grab her. She disappeared around the tunnel corner as the trolls entered the center cavern.

Solomon growled, and Dorothy hugged him tighter, stepping quietly back up the tunnel path.

"Who let the cat out?" said one of the voices.

A chorus of "not me's" chimed through the cave with each step Dorothy took.

"It's that cat from town!"

"There is no cat from town that could hurt Mum's cat like that," another voice said, exasperated.

"You've never been bit by Mum's cat! You don't know what those bite marks look like! It was one of those humans' cat!"

"What creature, especially from the human world, would ever attack Mum's cat? None, that's what.

Now, enough of your jittery jitters. Come on. I want to introduce you to my bride. I have been trying to catch her for years."

The trolls' bare feet slapped against the stone again and disappeared down one of the tunnels. When the light and voices had faded, Dorothy crept from the shadows and searched for the remnants of the firelight.

She had almost missed this tunnel. It was much smaller than the rest, and its entrance was just inside another tunnel, hidden behind a tattered cloth.

Solomon poked his head out of Dorothy's coat. The woman kissed his head and hugged him tight.

"Don't you ever run off on me again, you crazy cat."

Solomon purred softly and pushed into her chin. He jumped from her arms, this time waiting for her to pick up his leash. With his tail held high, he followed after the trolls and the bright orange light ahead.

TWELVE

IT WAS THE WORST IDEA SHE COULD HAVE possibly thought of. Following her cat into certain death. Why had she brought him? Why hadn't she at least put him back into her car before continuing on? But it was too late. They were too deep into the trolls' mountain.

Solomon's tail had experienced various stages of floof as they followed the trolls' voices through the winding tunnel. After what felt like a mile, Dorothy saw brackets and lit torches along the stone walls, with little shafts at the very top that seemed to be some kind of ventilation. It wasn't enough to get rid of the smell that permeated and grew stronger the deeper they went.

"Here are the lovely brides!" one of the voices said, and Dorothy stopped.

Solomon pulled against the leash, but she held him tight.

"We're not marrying you!" said a defiant, young voice.

The trolls chuckled, and Solomon's fur bristled. Even the hair on Dorothy's arms stood on end.

"You will do as you are told or end up as a bone broth!"

"Leave them alone! They are children."

Dorothy gasped. It was Hulda. Solomon's ears twitched back and forth at the sound of her voice. He pulled against the harness again, but Dorothy kept a tight grip.

"You are a brave one," said one of the trolls. "You have always been brave, Hulda."

"Don't touch me! And don't you dare say my name."

"I have enjoyed the sound of your name falling from my lips for longer than you can imagine. As soon as my brothers have found their brides, you will finally be mine."

"She is a feisty one, brother," said another troll. "Are you sure you can handle her?"

"Sometimes the glass just needs a little polish to see what is on the other side. With time, she will learn. With time, they all will learn."

"I will never accept you," Hulda spat.

Dorothy heard the children gasp. There was movement, and one of the girls began to cry.

"When the seasons have passed over and over again, when the walls begin to feel as though they are closing in around you. When you feel as though you cannot breathe, and you cannot remember the last time you saw the sun. Then, you will learn. You will learn that I have loved you since the moment I set eyes on you. You will not cower at my touch, and you will learn to love me, Hulda, as I have loved you."

There was a loud THWACK, and the trolls' laughter echoed through the cave once more.

"She showed you, brother," said one, rolling with laughter.

"Almost knocked your nose all the way to Christmas!" said another.

"Silence!" said the troll who had spoken to Hulda, though this voice was muffled.

"Come. We'll get some ice."

"For your nose, and that love-swollen brain of yours."

The laughter and footsteps faded once more, but Dorothy did not move. She waited in the shadows and darkness, just in case one remained behind.

"Your stubbornness could get you killed, Hulda," said a familiar voice.

Solomon's ears pricked forward, and he pulled at the leash again. This time, Dorothy obliged.

They emerged into the largest cave they had yet seen. Another tunnel continued on the far side of the room. But along the edges, the stalactites and stalagmites had formed a prison, behind which was Hulda, the missing children, and Caprice.

Solomon ran to the cage, and the children shrank back, stifling screams.

"Dorothy?" Caprice asked. Her clothes were dirty, and her face was gaunt. She stood, shielding the children behind her as both Dorothy and Solomon approached.

Solomon slid easily between the stone spires and leapt into Caprice's arms.

"Solomon?" she said.

"Caprice," Dorothy said, relieved to have found her friend and colleague at least.

"How did you get in here undetected?" Caprice asked.

"Very carefully," Dorothy said, keeping her voice low.

"How are you speaking Icelandic?" Hulda asked.

Dorothy furrowed her brow. "I – I'm not."

"It must be something to do with crossing through the magical barrier," Caprice said, setting Solomon at her feet.

The little cat stiffened, and his pupils dilated. Dorothy watched his fur bristle as Caprice held him.

"Don't you know it's rude to enter someone's home without their permission?"

Dorothy spun around, her hand flying to her hip where she had secured her gun. Before her towered a creature she had only seen in story books. A thin, humanoid creature with tufts of white hair and sagging, wrinkled skin. His fingers were long, ending in pointed, yellow nails that matched his pointed, yellow teeth. His clothes were well-kempt, though Dorothy didn't want to know where he had gotten the pale leather for his boots.

She pulled the gun from her belt, aiming between the troll's bright blue eyes.

"Don't you know it's rude to take things that don't belong to you?"

The troll laughed. "English? Now that is a tongue I have not heard in a long time. Though your accent is more American than British. Somewhere among your thirteen colonies?"

Dorothy shifted uncomfortably and adjusted her grip on her gun. "None of these people belong to you. Set them free, and you will remain unharmed."

The troll smiled and shook his head. "You humans

always were too bold for your britches. I can assure you, we have saved our brides."

"Saved them? From what?" Caprice asked.

"Are you so ignorant you cannot see what you are doing to your own world? Hulda, I will not hold you prisoner, but you will forever be immortal once you are wed to me. You will watch the destruction of your world. You will witness its people dying. And when there are no more flowers or rainbows, when there is no one left but me, you will see that I have saved you from the most horrific death."

"You would hold me here to watch everything I love be taken from me?" Hulda asked. "You would ask these children to watch their families grow old and die and be powerless to ever join them in peace? They are children. They are too young to endure such burdens. You will drive them mad!"

"They are free to live with their families. They have the power to grow as old as they wish, but, in the end, the true end, they will be safe."

"It is not for you to decide their fate," Caprice said softly. "Let them go. Show them mercy. Show them kindness. They may return to you of their own accord with time."

The troll was silent, his eyes landing on the group of children huddled in the corner of the makeshift prison.

"Gluggagægir, let them go, and I'll stay."

"Hulda, no!" said Dorothy.

"There is nothing left for me in the mortal world. And immortality will give me time to find my daughter."

Dorothy glanced at Hulda and saw her quickly wink. Hulda reached down and scratched at her hip, then turned back to the troll. Dorothy followed her gaze and gesture.

Sure enough, a set of keys dangled from Gluggagægir's belt. Dorothy's head swiveled back and forth until she found a door shrouded in the shadows that opened into the prison.

"You would do this?" Gluggagægir asked. "You would stay with me of your own choosing?"

"If you let the girls go," Hulda said, nodding.

"Gluggagægir!" The voice was unlike any Dorothy had yet heard. The sound of it alone made her fight every instinct in her to run. She felt her body tighten, and her hands began to shake.

Gluggagægir's eyes widened as well. He turned toward the second tunnel entrance. The keys on his hip were closer to Dorothy now.

Solomon gave a low growl as the sound of bare feet slapped against the stone, followed by the click of claws.

Dorothy's legs felt like jelly, but she stepped toward Gluggagægir, one hand still holding tight to her gun, the other reaching for the keys.

"I – I'm coming, Mother," said Gluggagægir.

"You are keeping secrets, Gluggagægir," said the voice again.

The troll turned back to Hulda, his face as terrified as Dorothy felt. "You must stay quiet," he whispered, heading toward the terrifying voice, the keys still jingling at his side.

Dorothy didn't wait. She ran to the door of the prison. It was carved with the same Nordic runes and pictures of what she assumed were the Yule Lads. She pulled on the handle, but it did not move, as she'd expected.

"It won't budge. I've tried," whispered Caprice.

"Can you pick the lock?" Hulda asked, joining the pair.

Caprice shook her head. "I haven't had anything to try with, but my guess is Hurðaskellir himself made this door. We aren't getting through it without those keys."

"I want Mommy!" one of the youngest girls said as she began to cry. One of the older children ran to her and covered her mouth with her hand.

"Hush!" she said. "We have to stay quiet."

Solomon's fur began to bristle again, and they heard the click of claws on stone once more.

Dorothy turned back to the tunnel entrance, her gun aimed into the darkness. A pair of yellow, glowing eyes caught in the torchlight of the room. A growl, much deeper than Solomon's, seemed to vibrate the entire room itself. The eyes blinked, and a large paw entered the room, bringing with it a cat that was larger than any bear Dorothy had ever encountered.

It circled the outside of the room, its mouth opened in a silent hiss. The little girl began to cry again, and the Yule cat screamed.

It stepped toward the Dorothy, its paw raised to strike. Solomon leapt through the stone bars, standing his ground between Dorothy and the Yule cat. He hissed and growled, his green eyes meeting the Yule cat's in challenge.

Dorothy stood frozen. If she fired at the Yule cat, she would be alerting the trolls to her presence – including Gryla. If she moved toward Solomon, she was sure the giant cat would attack her.

Solomon's leash still trailed behind him. She reached her foot out, stepping on the end. If she could slide the leash beneath her foot, she might be able to pull Solomon back to her.

Slowly, she slid her foot forward until it touched the

end of the leash. Solomon's growls had intensified, but neither he nor the Yule cat made a move. Dorothy lifted the toe of her foot and pivoted on her heel, coming to rest just on the end of the leash. The Yule cat hissed, and its breath smelled like death and decay. She slid her foot back, this time with the leash pressed beneath it. The moment Solomon felt tension on his harness, he jumped, lunging at the Yule cat.

"Solomon! No!" Dorothy cried.

Solomon latched on to the Yule cat's neck, biting and clawing at the giant creature. The Yule cat reared, trying to shake Solomon loose, but the little cat held on, blood dripping from his mouth.

"Get back!" Dorothy called to the prisoners. They fled to the far side of the cage, Caprice and Hulda shielding the children behind them. Dorothy aimed at one of the thinnest stalagmites and emptied her gun at it. The stone shattered and cracked but still held.

"Everyone, push!" Caprice led the way, leaning against the stalagmite. They heard it cracking, but it wasn't enough.

Dorothy turned back to the Yule cat. Solomon had edged down the creature's face and was hanging dangerously close to its mouth. She grabbed a chunk of stone and whipped it as hard as she could at the creature. It landed squarely on its throat. The giant cat screamed louder and shook its head. Solomon lost his grip and fell to the ground.

Without hesitation, the Yule cat lunged for Solomon. His teeth snapped around the cat's tail. Dorothy watched in horror as Solomon was flung through the air and slammed into the wall. He slid to the ground motionless, his tail now bent at an awkward angle.

With a loud CRACK, the stalagmite spire to the prison finally gave way. It shattered on the floor, startling the Yule cat. It hissed and growled and shook its head as dust rose through the air.

"Come on!" Hulda called. She hoisted the youngest girl onto her hip and ushered the children back through the tunnel.

"What's going on?" came one of the trolls' voices from the second tunnel.

"The brides!" another cried.

"Dorothy!" Caprice called.

Dorothy lifted Solomon into her arms and ran back up the tunnel.

The girls were already out of breath. Isabelle tripped and fell, and Caprice lifted her into her arms without missing a beat. She reached for one of the torches and handed it to Hulda, who still led the way.

"Who has been playing in my mountain?" Gryla's voice trailed behind them as they ran. "You bring toys into my mountain without telling me?"

"They are not toys, Mother. They are our brides."

"Look what they have done to my cat!"

The voices faded as the group continued through the tunnel. Solomon remained lifeless in Dorothy's arms. But there wasn't time to assess whether or not he was still alive.

"I can't keep going," one of the girls said, dropping to her knees.

"Yes, you can," said the oldest girl, pulling the first to her feet. "You have to. We're almost there."

They emerged into the main cavern. The girls looked around frantically, trying to find an exit.

"Which way? How do we get out of here?" one asked.

"This way!"

They all turned, and the torchlight landed on the figure of Ada, standing guard to one of the tunnels.

"Ada!" Dorothy said. "I thought you left."

"Just come on! Hurry!" Ada said.

"Come back!" called a voice through one of the tunnels. They heard the trolls' bare feet again, hurrying toward them.

Without a word, they bolted down Ada's tunnel.

"They're getting away!" another said.

The voices and stomping were coming closer.

"Do not leave!" one of the trolls said, his voice desperate and pleading.

"Hulda!" Gluggagægir said.

Dorothy turned. The trolls were almost within reach of them. The entrance was just ahead, and glorious sunlight was just beginning to break over the horizon.

They burst through the portal, the snow slowing their progress even more. Dorothy stumbled and held Solomon's body close to her chest as she fell.

"Now!" Ada cried.

Dorothy turned in time to see two of the trolls run out of the rock face. They threw up their hands, their faces twisted in agony as the sun bounced off dozens of mirrors held by the townsfolk.

The snow around the trolls' feet began to melt as their flesh smoked.

"Hulda, my love," Gluggagægir's strangled voice said before he turned entirely to stone.

The townsfolk cheered, and the girls ran to their parents. Dorothy took a deep breath and looked at the little cat lying still in her arms.

THIRTEEN

DOROTHY WATCHED SOLOMON'S CHEST RISE and fall. She hugged him close and heard a soft mew.

"Oh, Solomon," she whispered, her tears soaking his fur. "You stupid, *stupid* cat. I love you."

"Is he all right?" Caprice asked, kneeling beside Dorothy.

Dorothy lifted her head and nodded. "He's alive. But he needs a vet."

"I don't know how quickly we'll find one out here," Caprice said.

Dorothy swallowed hard as Caprice rose, her gaze fixed on the sky.

Dorothy heard the sound before she saw anything. She turned and watched a black speck in the sky grow larger and larger. The entire town that was still gathered on the mountainside watched in silence.

The parents clutched at their children again, and the children clung tight in return.

"*Vá! Það er þyrla,*" one of the children said, pointing at the sky.

"A helicopter?" Ada said. Dorothy hadn't noticed the girl standing behind her.

"It's heading straight for us." Dorothy quickly stood.

A murmur of suspicion and fear ran through the crowd as the helicopter flew closer.

"Artie?" Caprice said and pushed her way to the front of the crowd.

Unwilling to run closer to the mountain or the stone trolls, the townsfolk scattered, running down the mountain with their children on their backs or in their arms as the helicopter hovered directly over them. In the morning sun, Dorothy could make out a silver fox painted on its nose. It landed gracefully in the snow. The doors flew open, and both Artie and Destin leapt out.

Caprice ran to Destin. She fell into his arms and grabbed his face between her hands, kissing him.

"Fennec," Destin said, turning to Dorothy.

"What are you doing here?" Dorothy asked.

"I told you I was working on getting another agent to you," he said with a grin.

"You? I didn't know –"

"What? You didn't know I was also an agent?" He chuckled and hugged Caprice to his side. "When you didn't answer your calls, I got worried."

"Destin, I – I'm sorry, but…" She gently pulled Solomon away from her chest. He exhaled a deep, pitiful cry, and Dorothy felt her stomach sink. "He fought the Yule cat so we had a chance to free the girls."

Destin's eyes widened. He ushered Dorothy beneath the helicopter's blades and gestured for her to climb inside.

"Artie!" he called. "We have a Code Nebula. Agent down!"

Artie sprang into action. He looked at Dorothy, then noticed the little cat in her arms.

"I'm on it, Destin," he said, jumping into the helicopter.

"I'll call ahead," Destin said. "You can land right at Bráðamóttaka. Ask for Dr. Jon."

Artie nodded. He reached over Dorothy and slid the door closed. A hand stopped the door and quickly shoved it open again.

Hulda jumped inside and leaned between the two front seats.

"I am coming with you," she said.

Artie turned to Dorothy, who nodded and closed the door.

"Where are we going?" Dorothy asked.

Artie held up a finger for her to wait. He pulled a set of large headphones from beneath the seat and set them on her head. He pushed a button and asked, "Can you hear me?"

"Yes. Where are we going? Solomon –"

"We're taking him to the hospital," Artie said, handing another headset to Hulda.

Dorothy fumbled with the seatbelt, trying to hold on to Solomon. Hulda reached over and buckled her in before securing herself in one of the rear seats.

"The hospital? No, I'm fine. He needs a vet."

Artie nodded and began checking the controls. "Destin's calling in a Code Nebula. Dr. Jon will take care of Solomon."

"Who's Dr. Jon?"

Artie didn't answer. He gave Destin a thumbs up out of the window, and Destin returned it. Artie flicked another switch, and the helicopter began to rise into the air.

The ride wasn't nearly as smooth as the Learjet Dorothy had become accustomed to, but she took little notice. Solomon's breathing had become more rapid. It felt like hours when they finally landed on the roof of a hospital. A crew of security guards and a large, dark-skinned man stood waiting.

Hulda slid the door open, and the doctor ran forward.

"I'm Dr. Jon," the man said, his voice ringing with a surprising deep Irish accent. "What happened? Was it an artifact?"

Dorothy barely had time to breathe as the stranger took Solomon into his arms.

"He was attacked by the Yule cat," Hulda said.

The man nodded and called over his shoulder to a nurse who stood waiting in a doorway. "I'll take care of him. I promise." he said and took off toward the hospital.

Dorothy stood frozen, watching as the man sped off across the helipad, Solomon cradled in his arms. She felt an arm curl itself around hers. She looked at Hulda, her eyes blurred with tears.

"I need to go back for Destin and Caprice," Artie said from her other side. "He'll be all right. Dr. Jon's the best."

"Come on," Hulda said, pulling Dorothy toward the door.

"Agent Fennec?" said one of the security guards who stood waiting.

"Yes?" Dorothy asked.

The man nodded and ushered the pair inside. He led them through several hallways until Dorothy was utterly lost. Finally, he opened the door to an office suite, its lights still dim.

"You can wait here," the man said. "Dr. Jon will speak with you when he has finished."

He closed the door behind them, and Dorothy collapsed into a chair.

"He's going to be fine," Hulda said as she hugged the woman. "He is brave and strong."

"And stupid," Dorothy spluttered.

Hulda smiled. "He is bullheaded. Like someone else I know."

Dorothy grabbed an entire box of tissues from the desk in front of her. She pulled at least four out and blew her nose, not caring that it didn't sound the least bit dainty. She took several deep breaths and dried her tears.

"He's my last connection to Frank. My husband. My late husband. He's all I have left." Hulda nodded, and Dorothy saw she held the golden locket in her hand again. It must have fallen from Dorothy's pocket when she fell. "Oh, Hulda, listen to me. Blubbering about my cat when you – when Ann –"

Hulda shook her head. "Ann is still out there, I know it. It is a relief to know she's not the prisoner of Gluggagægir. If she is anything like her mother, she will give whoever has her Hell until I find her."

"Never stop looking, Hulda. Never stop."

Hulda smiled at Dorothy and squeezed her hands. "Never."

Dorothy slept the entire plane ride from Reykjavík back home. Solomon lay curled in her lap, refusing to leave her side. His tail had been bandaged, and though he had a large section of fur shaved him his side, Dr. Jon had used some artifact to quickly heal whatever internal damage the Yule cat had done.

Destin and Caprice slept in the chairs across from Dorothy, their arms draped around each other. She couldn't help but wonder what other secrets the man had hidden from her.

As the plane landed at the military base airport, they spoke little. Destin helped Artie unload the suitcases and kissed Caprice before she climbed into the taxi with Dorothy.

"You didn't abandon me to die in that troll's prison," Caprice said. "I just want to make sure you get home safe." She scratched beneath Solomon's chin and kissed his nose.

"I'm proud of you," Caprice said as the taxi merged onto the highway.

"For what?" Dorothy asked.

"For solving the case. I know it wasn't easy for you."

Dorothy smirked. "Well, the language barrier was definitely interesting, but I had help."

"Indeed," Caprice said, continuing to rub Solomon's chin.

The taxi parked in front of a giant snowdrift outside the little antique shop. The driver pulled Dorothy's suitcase out and helped her lug it over the snow.

"Can I get you a coffee or tea?" Dorothy asked as she unlocked the door.

Solomon bounded in, swishing his slightly kinked tail through the air. It would always have a slight bend to it now.

"No, I'll be fine. Destin's waiting for me back at the airport."

"I didn't know – about –"

Caprice laughed. "About me and Destin? That's the way it should be. Take it from me, Dorothy – subtlety is your best policy within the Silver Foxes."

Dorothy nodded, shedding her coat and laying it across the counter. Aaron had left the stack of mail on the edge for her, along with a business card. She had almost forgotten about the stranger. The card was plain, save for a phone number, just as Aaron had said.

"Is everything all right?" Caprice asked.

Dorothy snapped out of her thoughts and set the

card back on the counter. "Yes, I'm sorry."

Caprice picked up the card from the counter and squinted at it. She quickly set it down, turning to Dorothy.

"Dorothy, have you been asking questions about the Silver Foxes?" she asked.

Dorothy took a step back. "What? No. I've been trying to get my father's health records released."

Caprice shook her head. "Nothing this man says to you is true. Don't waste your time."

"How do you know who this is? It's just a phone number."

"Because he's been poking his nose around the Silver Foxes for longer than you can imagine. He's a liar and a thief. Do not trust him."

Solomon wound himself around Dorothy's ankles and pawed at her pant leg. She picked him up and stared at the card.

"I need to know what happened to my father, Caprice. Destin refuses to tell me, and the United States Department of Inquiry seems to have the information under lock and key for some reason. Don't you find that odd?"

"For your own protection, for Aaron's and Red's, for Solomon's, do not contact that man."

Caprice leaned in and hugged both Dorothy and

Solomon. Her grip was still weakened from her time kept in captivity with the trolls.

"Call me if you need anything," she said, letting herself out.

Dorothy watched as Caprice climbed back into the taxi and drove away. She snatched the card off the counter and headed to her apartment behind the avocado-green door.

She opened a tin of food for Solomon and sat in her chair, the card in one hand, and her phone in the other. A little green light flashed at the top of the phone, and Dorothy swiped to unlock it.

Three missed calls from Mary Pat. She immediately dialed her sister.

"Hello?" Mary Pat answered.

"Mary Pat, it's Dorothy," Dorothy said, immediately pulling the phone away from her ear.

"Dory-dear! I was just thinking about you! You know, I tried calling you, but I thought you might still be swept away somewhere with that man of yours."

"What? No, I was traveling on business," Dorothy said as Solomon climbed on her lap.

"Of course, you were, dear. Now, what can I do for you?"

"You called me three times. Just a half hour ago."

"Oh, yes! I called that United American States

Department of Inquisition for you," Mary Pat said. Dorothy rolled her eyes.

"You mean United States Department of Inquiry? Please tell me you called the right one."

"Yes, yes. It was the right one. Anyway, they wouldn't tell me a thing about Daddy. Then this man called. Some Robbie Hodge."

"Robbie Hodge?" Dorothy asked, looking at the card in her hand.

"Do you know him, Dory-dear?"

"What did he say, Mary Pat?"

"He wanted to know the strangest thing. He wanted to know if I knew anything about foxes. Imagine such a thing. I told him I donate to the Metroparks every year, and I wasn't going to be scammed out of any money."

"You didn't," Dorothy breathed.

"Oh, I did. I told him I was an intelligent woman, and he wasn't going to play me. And I hung up on him."

Dorothy heard Mary Pat slap the arm of her chair. She sighed, and Solomon gave her arm a gentle kiss.

"So, you didn't learn anything about Dad's health records, then?"

"Oh, I learned a great deal, Dorothy. Don't sell me so short. That Department of Inquisition place is top-level security. I don't know why they would have Daddy's healthy records."

"What do you mean top level? How do you know that?"

"The sounds, Dorothy. Really, now. There was a scratchy sort of silence after I called, followed by a beep that you wouldn't be able to hear normally. But I had my hearing aid turned up all the way that day. They were recording the conversation, and they didn't tell me. Then I heard that sort of beep from a security badge in the background while I was talking to someone. They shuffled me around a bit, but each person I talked to seemed to know more and more about me, even though they tried to play dumb about it. I can read their voices, Dory."

"That could have been any government place you called, Mary Pat."

"Well, I might agree with you, except the next day, I had a new delivery boy bring me my groceries. See, I know all the personal shoppers down at the Super Value."

"They could have hired someone new," Dorothy said.

"Perhaps, but whenever they hire someone knew, they always follow policy to a T. You know, they get a raise every thirty days for the first ninety days if they have no incidents or complaints. This man was older than any of the kids they're hiring for the job these days. He insisted on bringing my groceries into the kitchen and helping me put things away. But I told him *no*. I told him I didn't want him to miss out on his raise, and his eyes said he had no idea what I was talking about."

Dorothy sighed again. Sometimes *she* had no idea what Mary Pat was talking about. "Well, I appreciate you calling and trying, Mary Pat."

"It's no trouble, dear. Now, you sound like you just rolled in off a plane. You get some sleep. I'll chat with you soon."

Mary Pat ended the call before Dorothy could. She was relieved. Her sister could drone on with nonsense for hours if someone let her.

Dorothy looked at the card still clutched in her hand. She turned to Solomon, who stared at her with his bright green eyes.

"What do you think, little one?" she asked.

Solomon stood. He turned in a circle and rubbed against the phone she had set on the arm of the chair. It fell to the floor, and Solomon lay down with a huff.

Dorothy smiled and gently stroked his coat, careful to avoid his still-healing tail. She'd call in the morning.

FOURTEEN

FOUR MONTHS LATER

THE CHILDREN WAITED PATIENTLY ON THE merry-go-round for Dorothy to get settled on her usual bench. They approached quietly, though their energy buzzed with excitement. They immediately dropped to the ground, and Solomon flopped over, welcoming the pets and giggles.

"Can we take him on the swing again?" one of the little girls asked.

Dorothy handed her the leash. "Only if he wants to. Just make sure I can see him and you."

The children squealed with laughter and took off for the swing sets, Solomon trotting behind them. She watched as they patted the seat to one of the baby swings, encouraging Solomon to jump on. The little cat made sure to rub on the shins of each child before obliging and jumped onto the seat.

The children laughed, some jumping up and down with excitement. Solomon sat down, his kinked tail sticking out one of the leg holes. He seemed to smile as the children took turns gently pushing him on the swing. It had become an almost-daily occurrence since spring break had begun.

Dorothy smiled and watched as a stranger joined her at the other end of the bench.

"Your cat is quite the celebrity around here," he said.

Dorothy nodded, her smile deepening as she watched the little cat playfully bat the children each time he swung close. "He's very special," she said.

"I appreciate you taking the time to call me, even if it took you months to do so," the man said.

"I had other obligations," Dorothy said, not taking her eyes of Solomon and the children.

"You mean other missions," the man said, his voice sly. "I admit, I was surprised you thought to use someone else's phone."

"One can't be too careful."

"I suppose you're right. Then again, meeting in broad daylight may not have been the best call."

Dorothy swallowed and felt her face blush. She took a drink from her water bottle, making a point to carefully recap it before replying, "Who are you, Mr. Hodge?"

"I am a curious mind, like yourself. I am an investigator and a protector."

"Some say you're a liar and a traitor," Dorothy said, raising an eyebrow at the man.

"Some, or just the Foxes?"

Dorothy didn't answer. She watched as the children led Solomon to the merry-go-round and pretended to parade him at a show.

"Do you know how Richard died, Ms. Claes?" Mr. Hodge asked.

"Do you?" Dorothy asked.

"I know his official cause of death is listed as old age. That is not a modern diagnosis. Why do you think that is?"

"My father *was* very old. He passed in his sleep, though his internal organs showed no signs of failure."

"And you don't find this odd?"

Dorothy sighed and turned to the man beside her. "Do you think I would have contacted you if I didn't?"

The man flashed a smile. He was in his fifties with perfectly straight teeth and bright blue eyes. His blond hair was slicked back like Destin's, though it fell across his face in a roguish sort of way.

"I'll release your father's health records, Ms. Claes.

No questions asked. Just one condition."

"Name it," Dorothy said.

"Leave the Silver Foxes immediately."

ABOUT THE AUTHOR

C.P. Morgan, or Cassandra Penelope Morgan, was born in a small town in Ohio. She comes from a family of both writers and English majors from both sides of her family.

The idea for the Silver Fox Mysteries was inspired by stories she heard growing up about her grandmothers. She also writes YA Fantasy under the name Cassandra Morgan.

Cassandra is a frequent guest at conventions and writing conferences in the Midwest area. She is a writing coach, a foster for orphaned kittens, and participates with The International Cat Association.

Connect with Cassandra!

WWW.AUTHORCASSANDRAMORGAN.COM
WWW.AUTHORCPMORGAN.COM
CONTACT@AUTHORCASSANDRAMORGAN.COM

FACEBOOK: **/author.cassandra.morgan**
TWITTER: **@AuthorCasMorgan**
INSTAGRAM: **@Morgan_Cassandra**